TRUE DEDICATION

TRUE DEDICATION

HAWTHORN ACADEMY BOOK NINE

D.R. PERRY

THE TRUE DEDICATION TEAM

Thanks to our JIT Readers

Rachel Beckford
Dave Hicks
Veronica Stephan-Miller

Editor
SkyHunter Editing Team

LMBPN Publishing
PMB 196, 2540 South Maryland Pkwy
Las Vegas, NV 89109

Version 1.00, September 2021
(Previously published as a part of the megabook *Hawthorn Academy: Year Three*)
ebook ISBN: 978-1-68500-450-7
Print ISBN: 978-1-68500-451-4

CHAPTER ONE

On my first day back on campus, I sent Ember around with messages for the team, asking them to meet in the gym after lunch. Alex arrived first, and the pit of my stomach dropped. He walked right up to me and stood with his arms crossed as though he dared me to admit I'd made a mistake. To avoid embarrassing him, I dealt with his situation before everyone else showed.

I tried telling myself Coach Pickman might be wrong. Despite what I'd overheard during break, maybe his mom would let him come to extra practice. I wasn't wearing ear cuffs.

You already know the answer without asking.

I extended the invitation anyway.

"No way, Morgenstern." He tilted his chin up, trying his best to look down his nose at me. "Impossible."

"Remember, you'll be welcome if, uh, things change."

"Why don't you change the location to here, then?" He snorted.

I said nothing, just pulled the jewelry box out of my pocket and showed it to him.

"We're both shackled then." His brow furrowed. "I'm not sure which of us has the harsher jailer."

"It's not a contest." I sighed and returned the box to my blazer.

"Anyway, I can run extra drills and give you notes in the gym on a different day."

"Coach has to be there." He sniffed. "For...reasons."

"Okay, let's talk schedule, and I'll make it happen." I got out my notebook.

He rattled off his work hours, and I jotted them down. As we finished, Dylan sauntered through the door. He stopped at the bleachers, apparently tying his shoe. Alex turned his back and took a step away from me before pausing.

"Thanks, Morgenstern."

"No problem, Alex."

"My mother calls me that." He looked over his shoulder. "It's Xan."

"Xan then. See you later."

Dylan didn't approach until the door closed. I glanced down at his shoes, which were new, and noticed something interesting.

"Those are slip-on. No laces."

"Right. Christmas present. Mum's doing well here." He cleared his throat. "I remember the work-study shuffle. Is that going to hinder him, what with all the extra practices?"

"No."

"It's not work though."

"What did you see?"

"Big green miasma. What did you hear?"

"Discord. He's in trouble."

"Surely not as bad as last year, with Intemperance?"

"No. Not as bad. But different."

"Bollocks. What should we do?"

"I'm not sure. We need more information."

"I'll keep my eyes peeled if you put your ears on the walls."

"Did Noah give you a Ted Talk on snark?"

"I wish." He sighed.

"If you like him, say something."

"Noah must need something more grandiose than a plain declaration."

"I've known him most of his life, Dylan." I grinned. "Don't posture or make him think you're waiting for an answer. Just put your feelings out there. He's cautious, takes his time. But he can't choose something if he's got no idea it's even an option."

"So I'm not super obvious, then?"

"Only to the mind magus."

"Aces." He slapped his hand over his mouth. "Sorry."

"It's cool."

The rest of the team arrived, all carrying beverages. I made the announcement and gave them the schedule. Nobody asked about Xan, so I added that information at the end, including his nickname.

Might be a mistake. If his mother was right and nobody really cares what happens to him.

Someone did, though. One of my teammates lingered after everyone else had gone.

"Can I come to those extra drills?" Lee tapped one foot against the hardwood.

"Sure. Once I know exactly when they are."

"Good." He nodded, then turned on his heel and stalked out of the gymnasium, leaving me with my thoughts. I took off along the track, trying to outrun them.

I showered before dinner, of course, putting on pajamas afterward because nobody much cared what we wore in the cafeteria on Sundays. Dorian stood outside the door to my room.

"Can I come in?"

"If you don't mind me drying my hair."

"That doesn't bother me."

Grace had left a note on my desk saying her stomach couldn't wait. I put my basket of toiletries away and sat with my hairbrush on my bed, leaving the chair for Dorian. He stood blinking at me.

"What's up?"

"Don't you need a hairdryer?"

"No." I smiled and held up my hands. "I use magic for that. So what can I do for you?"

"First of all, thanks."

"Hmm?" I held the brush in one hand and put the other over it as I went over my hair, conjuring a small amount of solar energy to help it dry.

"For going out of your way to include Xan. Not holding a grudge."

"Don't thank me for being a decent human. You're the one who's really helping. Inviting him ho—"

"Shh." He swallowed. "I think the walls have ears."

"Yeah." I sighed. "Okay. You're really kind to him."

"I wanted to ask, because of the mind magic, I mean. Do you know if it's helping? Like, are things getting better for him?"

Don't say one word about them spending break together. You've got no idea who knows what. And he's right about the walls.

I closed my eyes and tried to sense my surroundings beyond what the voice said. Sure enough, a mild hum came from the wooden walls. What sort of magic energy had caused it, I couldn't tell.

He's waiting for an answer.

"He's not the same as he was last year. But Dorian, I haven't interacted with him enough to say for sure what the changes mean. I think the best thing to do is wait and let him show us."

"What about your first year?" He studied his fingers, which he'd locked together in front of him. "Because I wasn't there for that. And yeah, I've heard the rumors."

"The only things I see in him now from back then are mannerisms." My hair was dry, so I set the brush on my nightstand.

"I guess you're right." Dorian nodded. "Anyway, are you ready for dinner?"

"Sure, let's go."

The week passed much like the ones before winter break, for class and regular Bishop's Row practice anyway. The sessions with Mr.

Fairbanks were as fraught with tension. Hal sat in his magic chair instead of the couch, revealing its reclining feature. On Friday in the lounge with our to-go dinners, I mentioned it, igniting an excited discussion about enhancements and applications for an entire fleet of them.

"You don't even have to worry whether there's stairs or ramps because of the levitation," Dylan said. "Faith's idea, but Hal invented the process."

"But I didn't invent physics," Hal protested.

"I bet you can add a wood magic enchantment." Lee nodded. "So the frame has a flexible size range for navigating different doorways."

"We could make them look any which way." Grace smiled. "Glamour and umbral enchantments would do that. I've been working on a color and pattern dial with Az for shoes. I bet it'd work on that too. How cool would it be to make the frame match your outfit?"

"That's amazing!" Kitty clapped her hands. "Have you considered heating and cooling? You already have water and air in there. Why not add heating and cooling so you're comfortable no matter what?"

"Awesome ideas, folks." Hal grinned.

"Use them, then," Eston said. "Build the best chair possible."

"I'll think about it. Incidentally, the engineering design was my entry in the local magipsych fair. I'll give those a try after it's scored in February." The grin faded. Mine followed.

He knows he won't have time. Not to do all that.

"Hey," I cleared my throat. "The team and the squad have extra practice at Salem State tomorrow at eight-thirty. I talked it over with Logan, and we don't mind an audience. So, come along. The more, the merrier."

The subject shifted to cheer squad, with Kitty and Logan asking opinions on music choices through the rest of dinner. Dorian kept recommending Weird Al songs that made everyone laugh even if they all got vetoed. Eventually, the lights went off behind the café counter.

"Guess that's our cue." Dylan jerked a thumb at the darkened area. He whistled for Gale. "Come on, buddy. Upstairs time."

The dragonet didn't respond. I turned to look up at the perch he'd been sitting on with Ember and found her missing, too.

"Oh no." I jumped out of my seat, stepped around the low table, and prepared to sprint off in search of her.

"Wait." Logan put a hand on my elbow. "Shh. I'm listening."

He tilted his head, stepping carefully toward the column by the doorway. It was shaped to look like a tree trunk, with the archway made in the likeness of a coniferous branch, needles and all. After a moment of standing beneath it, Logan beamed and pointed up. We all stood there staring, unable to see what he indicated until we walked to stand beside him. That's when we finally noticed the golden tail curling around from the lobby side of the decorative embellishment.

I stepped into the open space, still looking up. Nestled in the Y made by the stylized trunk and arching branch sat a nest. The bundles of dining hall napkins and scraps of fabric from Creatives mostly obscured her hindquarters, but Ember was clearly laying eggs.

"So much for that brooding box, eh?" Grace elbowed me.

"Yeah." I nodded.

"Are you surprised?" Grace asked.

"Not really." I sighed. "How are we going to move them down?"

"I'm in this with you, Aliyah." Dylan chuckled. "No trouble for an air magus."

"It's almost lights out though," Eston pointed out. "We'll get in trouble if we're not upstairs in a few minutes. Is it safe to move a dragonet nest that quickly?"

"You shouldn't move them tonight anyway," Logan added. "She might keep laying eggs for hours and moving them in the middle stresses the whole family. Actually, moving them at all might be a bad idea. We should check with Bubbe."

"How many do you think there are?" Kitty peered up, trying to get a better look. "I see two."

"Ember doesn't know, so neither do I." I shrugged.

"Move along now. I'm closing up." Xan strode out of the café's lounge, pointing at his apron. "Scram so I can clock out already."

"Don't have to tell me twice."

Dylan led the way toward the stairs, Hal bringing up the rear in his chair. I followed them halfway across the lobby before I realized Dorian wasn't with us.

He's not okay.

Sure enough, when I turned to look, he was back by the doorway and gazing up at the nest. His shoulders shook although no sound of sniffles or sobs carried across the space between us. Julia the strix swooped down from somewhere overhead. When she landed on his shoulder, he only shrugged her off, shooing her away. Dorian's bewildered familiar came to me instead, perching on my shoulder where she fluttered and hooted her dismay. I wasn't sure what to do for her at first. Owls didn't like being petted.

Just wait for it.

I let Julia use me as a perch and gave Dorian a few moments to compose himself, unsure why Ember and Gale making a nest had him so distraught.

Gryphons hatch. And Mercy was awfully young.

My stinging eyes erupted with full-blown tears when Xan emerged from the now darkened lounge and put his arms around Dorian. The pair turned to face each other, revealing how red Dorian's face was and the tender way Xan stroked his hair as they rocked back and forth. Now I could hear them, one sobbing as the other murmured.

Feeling like an intruder, I turned and got on the stairs, whispering our floor. Logan waited at the top. He took one look at Julia, nodded, then escorted me to Dorian's room where we waited with the strix. Five minutes later, Dorian showed up alone, eyes puffy but much more composed. Julia turned her head all the way around. He murmured a few words of thanks to us, then walked behind me. Logan followed.

"Sorry, Julia." He sighed. "There's no good excuse. I know you're grieving too."

She hooted, then clicked her beak twice.

"She says you owe her ten crickets," Logan said.

He shouldn't have translated that.

"Twenty, if you want."

"Well, isn't this interesting."

I turned to face Leo Pierce, who'd walked up behind the boys as they addressed Julia. The last thing I wanted was for him to witness Logan's rare ability. Especially after what I'd learned about his sister Petra in the yearbook. So I scrambled to cover for him.

"Yeah, mind magic has loads of cool features." I put on my best intimidating grin, the one I'd used so often last year during the social skirmishes with Temperance Fairbanks. "Great for amazing and astounding your friends."

"This is why nobody trusts the Morgensterns. You're all a pack of shysters." Mr. Pierce snorted. "And you're the most flagrant liar of the bunch. I happen to know mind magic doesn't work that way."

"She's an extramagus." Dorian stepped between Logan and his father. "Are you sure it doesn't work that way for her?"

"I always suspected this." He ignored Dorian. "You can't hide from me much longer, Logan. Not even behind your most powerful friends."

"Are you threatening me?" Logan's voice cracked.

"Not at all. I only want what's best for you, son." He turned his back and sauntered away down the hall. "And the rest of the family. Enjoy what little freedom you've got while it lasts."

Once he was gone, Dorian leaned against the wall.

"Gods, Logan. I'm sorry."

"Why?"

"I got you in trouble. Because I got all emo downstairs and left you all in the lurch."

"How my father acts isn't your fault." Logan cleared his throat. "Or mine. I blurted it on an official record by accident. So it was only a matter of time before he found out."

"Yeah, Dorian." I nodded. "Grief happens."

"Thanks." He held out his arm, and Julia hopped to it. "I'd better get some sleep before anything else goes wrong tonight."

"See you tomorrow?" I asked.

"At Salem State? Yeah, I'm recording practice for Xan. Goodnight."

"Goodnight."

I walked Logan to his room, not leaving until the door latched behind him. After that, I went to mine, where Grace already slept soundly. It took me what felt like an hour of tossing and turning before I slept too.

I got up earlier than I normally did for classes. Nobody else was around in the cafeteria, not even the kitchen staff. So I had instant oatmeal and black tea using the self-service hot water dispenser. The oatmeal was always out on the counter in a metal rack, along with the tea and coffee sweeteners. It took a few minutes for the grains to soak, so I searched unsuccessfully for a spoon.

Normally, I would have relied on Ember to hunt down an item like that. But on the way in, I'd caught a glimpse of her asleep in her nest. Instead of waking the broody dragonet, I added more water to my breakfast, cold this time, until it became a slurry I could drink from the cup. Not exactly pleasant, but nourishing.

Salem State was a mile and a half from that day's Hawthorn door beside the Peabody Essex Museum. I jogged, which kept me warm enough without any magic in only my sweats, a hat, and gloves. Most of the time, I enjoyed cozy clothes on winter mornings and the company of friends around town. However, I'd never been to the gym at Salem State University before. Arriving early and on my own would give me a chance to figure out how to use the space.

Because of this, I expected to be the first person inside. Maybe even be stuck outside for a few minutes, since I got there before six. I was wrong. A chunk of brick held the door open a crack so I widened it more to step over it and inside, where all the lights were on.

Someone in a hooded sweatshirt sat on the bleachers, surrounded by books. A blond man dribbled a basketball down the court, coming to a short stop before shooting a perfect two-point basket. The hooded person sat up, revealing her face and clearing her throat. It was Lynn Frampton, who I'd met at the college fair.

The man on the court straightened, then turned to face me. I knew this fellow, too.

"Bobby Tremain?"

"Yeah." He rubbed the back of his head with one hand with a sheepish grin as he held the other out. "Aliyah, right? Captain of Hawthorn's Bishop's Row team?"

"That's right." I nodded and shook his hand.

"Nice to see you again."

"My coach said her friend was going to help me out here."

"Oh, Coach Warren isn't a morning person. She sent me to open the doors and just kind of hang out."

"You're supervising Bobby," Lynn chided. "It's part of your Mass Ed certification. Or are you having second thoughts about that Gallows Hill PE position?"

"Yeah, no." Bobby chuckled. "I kind of understate stuff sometimes. Anyway, I'll show you where the locker rooms are. What kind of equipment do you need?"

I rattled off a list as we walked. The setup was similar to Hawthorn's with a gender-neutral locker room between two gendered ones but smaller. Equipment closets were off to the left of the women's. He opened one, revealing racks and hooks with sets of ballistae, cestus, and ankyr in various sizes. I thanked him, and he headed to the other side of the gym.

At first, I expected Bobby to go back to shooting hoops. He walked right past the ball, not stopping until he reached the opposite wall and opened a small panel, the sort that covers circuit breakers. Some of the switches inside glowed. He flipped those, then toggled a few more. In a moment, I understood.

Those were controls, magipsychic ones, that customized the lines on the court. Shifter-regulation basketball lines morphed into official Bishop's Row boundaries. The baskets folded back against the wall, and wards went up along the lines between the playing area and the bleachers.

Initially, I'd worried about space for both the Bishop's Row practice and the cheer squads. I shouldn't have. The court only took up half the gym, which had sacrificed locker room size for play area. Sensible, considering they were one of the first formerly mundane public universities to have shifter regulation sports.

The tea and oatmeal breakfast plus the jog over gave me an excuse to check out the locker rooms. There wasn't a lot of space for changing, the shower and toilet stalls were cramped, and luxury features like the sauna, steam room, and whirlpool bath weren't included here. A sign informed me they were at the sports medicine office around the corner outside. However, this place didn't need to be fancy, just inclusive enough for all of us to practice using our full abilities.

I hung my hat and gloves on a hook beside the lockers. The facilities were typical of mundane spaces, nothing special. Everything worked fine. After washing my hands, I left the locker room. Before I made it halfway across the gym, the door opened again signaling new arrivals.

It was Izzy, walking with Lee and a few Bishop's Row players from Messing. They chuckled together over cups of hot chocolate I could smell from where I stood. Still nervous, my stomach didn't envy their beverages. The only reservations I had about being such an early bird were for someone else. Should I have woken Logan, brought him along? I didn't like imagining him making the trek alone.

My worries vanished a moment later when he entered and stood holding the door open for Hal's chair. Everyone else from my year at Hawthorn walked in after that. Arick Magnuson showed up as well, a handful of second years following him with Lena bringing up the rear.

"Hey, Aliyah!" Dylan waved, then jogged over. "I saw Brianna out there with her team and Cadence with her squad. They'll be here in a minute."

"Thanks."

Once everyone was inside, I showed them the locker rooms. Logan and Cadence went back to talk to Bobby, who brought them to another closet. Inside were batons, pom-poms, and ribbons on sticks. I glanced back at the door, expecting to see more students. Kitty tapped me on the shoulder.

"Jacinda's not coming." She sighed and shook her head. "I asked, and she said her squad doesn't need extra practice."

"Oh." I swallowed. "I hope everything's okay."

"It is." Izzy nodded. "Basically, she thinks it's more auspicious to rehearse in the evenings."

"Is that a thing?"

"It is to her." Izzy shrugged. "Just know that it's got nothing to do with Logan."

"Are you sure?"

"She met a guy on vacation in Disney World. Dead ringer for Flynn Ryder, judging by the pic she showed me. Anyway, let's do this."

Izzy went to round up her teammates while Lee stuck with us. Elanor showed up, then had a few words with Bobby. He went out the door to the hallway where sports medicine was and returned with Noah, who'd arrived by tunnel.

All told, we had enough players total to run four teams, and Salem State's gym was large enough to accommodate two simultaneous games and still leave room for both cheer squads to practice. While Bobby changed the court markings and wards to make two courts, Izzy, Brianna, and I sorted all the players, working out a schedule to switch opponents.

One amazing thing about the morning was getting the chance to play with and against students from the other schools. It felt more fun than regular practice, providing challenges that felt fresher than drills and disjointed plays.

The best part was how it felt, playing as I'd done since first year without the ear cuffs. Instead of that dulled-down sense of tunnel vision I'd experienced on campus lately, I felt almost hyperaware and more connected to my team in general and the overall fun of the game.

Dorian recorded everything. Not with his phone as I'd expected, either, but a set of magipsychic cameras he'd checked out from Salem State's AV center. Hal helped, filming from his chair. I heard them talking during one of my water breaks.

"This is some amazing footage." Dorian smiled. "Like, pro sports network quality. Thanks, Hal."

"Make sure you show it off, then." Hal grinned. "After edits and stuff."

"That's the plan."

We had to be out of the gym by noon, so we wrapped practice at eleven-thirty. People shook hands, exchanged high fives, and headed off to the locker rooms tired but mostly smiling. Someone tugged at my sleeve. I turned to find Lena Zanelli.

"Thanks," she mumbled.

"No problem."

"Could've been. Micello's a beast. Now I know."

"You know?"

"Strategy." She tapped the side of her head. "Counters for glamour."

"We're doing it again in two weeks."

"Good." She nodded. "Thanks again, Captain."

Before I could insist she call me Aliyah, Lena strode away to the locker room.

"Wow." Arick stood nearby blinking. "That's more than she says in class when she's called on."

"Really?"

"Pretty much." He nodded. "Cadence went to clean up, but she wanted me to ask if Hawthorn and Messing want Engine House for lunch."

"I'll let everyone know, including Izzy. Thanks, Arick."

Hal, Faith, and Dorian headed back toward campus, but everyone else went out for lunch. I ordered a pizza to go for them, and caught up half a block later. Dorian saved his share, said he wasn't hungry. Later on, I saw him pass his pizza along to Xan.

CHAPTER TWO

We practiced every other Saturday at Salem State after that. Our audience changed sometimes, but the players stayed the same. Hal and Faith always left together instead of meeting up for lunch either on or off-campus. The second week, I spotted them halfway up the block from me on Hawthorne Street, stepping out of the driveway between my and Izzy's houses. It became a regular occurrence.

Bubbe never mentioned their visits, not even when I asked if she'd seen them lately. They separately made the same excuse to me. Vitamins for Nin and Seth. I knew that cover story well enough, but I trusted them both. If the reason for meeting with Bubbe ever became my business, they'd tell me.

Each Sunday, I met with Dorian and Xan at the gym on campus to go over the videos. Lena ended up tagging along, watching in silence as Xan asked questions. I'd expected anger or at least bitterness over being left out. If he bore any ill will, he didn't direct it at the rest of the team or me.

Letters trickled in from colleges and universities. Faith made early acceptance at Providence Paranormal College. Kitty got an offer at Virginia Magitech, but Eston didn't. Emerson College invited Dorian to an audition, but he received an early admissions academic rejection the next day. Everybody buckled down on studying, hitting the books harder than at any time besides exams last spring. We had dinner in the lounge every night, even on weekends, wolfing down food so we'd still have time to visit the library before lights out.

Logan's guarantee at Providence Paranormal didn't make him immune. He divided his time between translating Ludovico's journals and helping all of us. I worked hard too. My college application was regular rather than early admission but that didn't make slacking a good idea.

The only one of us not scrambling was Grace. Her plans didn't include a conventional extrahuman education path. Instead, she'd applied at Salem State for a mundane business degree. They had rolling admissions, so she wouldn't get rejected there.

"Don't you want to study more magic?" I asked one night before bed. "You're so good at theory, and your lab work is awesome."

"I want to run my own business." She shrugged. "I need to learn that part as soon as possible, or I could get into legal trouble."

"You're so practical."

"And you're not? You've got a knack for coaching. If you weren't set on extraveterinary, I'd expect to see you running a team someday."

I told her about my doubts and the Coast Guard.

"You're going to rock at any of those things, but you told me years ago about taking over Bubbe's practice. And Providence Paranormal."

"I'm not so sure anymore."

"Any particular reason?"

"Logan's better with critters than I am, and look at Faith. She's going pre-med when she used to be all about poly-sci."

"You want to be a doctor then." She nodded.

"Well, maybe. If I can get in, and if people would even trust their health to an extramagus."

"They trust vampire doctors, right?" She pulled the blanket to cover her shoulder. "Anyway, there's nothing wrong with changing your major. Start with general requirements in your first semester."

"You have a point." I yawned. "I'll figure it out eventually, I guess. Thanks, Grace. Goodnight."

"Night."

The Magipsych Fair was off-campus, in the Peabody Essex Museum's Atrium, and included the other area schools. The event was packed, but not with students presenting. We weren't required to submit projects. Messing students filled most of the tables, with seven projects on display. Gallows Hill only had two. Hawthorn brought three, two from second-year students and Hal's, which involved most of the third years.

Hal asked me to help fold and stow his table. Since the very chair he sat in was his project, he didn't want to hide it. After propping it against the wall, I turned to see a group of our friends heading toward us.

"How will you display your abstract, though?" Logan scratched his head. "All the data on the enchantments you tried before getting it just right?"

"Like this." Hal grinned and pressed a button on the chair's left arm.

A magipsychic projection expanded above his head, opening like a set of curtains on a stage. The data arrayed itself neatly, with a 3-D rendered image of the chair rotating as it assembled and disassembled itself.

"Wow." I smiled. "You already won."

"If this contraption places, then everyone's a winner."

"Hey, don't call it that." Dylan frowned. "Still think he needs a proper name."

"He vetoed Ellida." Faith shrugged. "No dragons, he said."

"How about Argo?" Dorian asked. "I mean, a moving chair is sort of like a ship."

"Why not have everyone write their ideas on paper and pull one out of a hat?" Eston said.

"I like that idea." Hal nodded. "Who's got stuff to write with?"

"Me!" Logan pulled a memo pad and stub of pencil out of his blazer pocket, but the tip was broken.

"Hang on." Kitty reached into her purse and pulled out an eyeliner sharpener.

"I've got this." Grace took off her mauve cloche hat and turned it upside-down.

"Better do it fast." Lee pointed across the room. "Judges headed this way."

Everyone took a turn with the paper and pencil, scrawling their ideas, tearing paper, and dropping them into the hat. The twins hurried over to join in. Grace passed the hat to Hal, who closed his eyes and rummaged. He opened them a second before unfolding the blue and white scrap.

"Okay. Who wrote Floaty McChairface?"

Silence reigned until Faith snorted. After that, everybody laughed.

"Just kidding." Hal smiled down at the paper. "This works." He opened a panel in the right armrest and keyed the word in. "I present Neshmet."

The chair's new name appeared on the display as the judges approached.

We let Hal do most of the talking, except when one of them asked a specific question. I hung back, cleaning up paper scraps along with Hailey and Bailey.

"We didn't really do anything, Aliyah," Hailey said. "You should be up there with the rest of them."

"The only thing I contributed was moral support."

"Still more than I did." Bailey sighed. "Feels like I wasted a lot of time. Now high school's almost over."

"It's never too late." Hailey elbowed her twin. "To make up for that, I mean."

Hailey was only partly correct.

Hal's wasn't the last project the judges looked at. When they returned ten minutes later, I rejoined the group because I knew before they said a word what had happened.

"Congratulations, Team Hawthorn." A diminutive woman with freckles, laugh lines, and salt and paprika hair extended her hand. "I'm

Doctor Smith. Your Neshmet chair won. We'd like to invite you all to the state fair this spring. If you haven't applied to MIT Mr. Hawkins, please consider it. I'm in charge of the magipsychic studies department there, and the enchantments are truly impressive. I can tell your leadership and personal experience were strong elements here."

"Thank you," Hal responded. "If some of us can't be at state, is that okay?"

"As long as at least one member of your team is present and able to answer questions like the ones tonight, that's acceptable." She nodded.

"I'm there, whatever happens." Faith reached for Hal's hand.

Something flashed as their fingers intertwined. Metal. Jewelry. Rings, a pair of them. Were they engaged?

"Sounds great." Hal gazed up at her, beaming. That smile lit up his entire face.

It was almost the last time I saw him wear any sort of joyful expression.

***

With how busy I'd been, preparing for the Valentine's Day dance felt like almost an afterthought. Grace wasn't anywhere near as enthusiastic about it as she'd been for any of the other dances. Although she brought each of her classmates outfits again, she laid a secret on me.

"It's almost all upcycling," she confessed. "I don't have the time I used to, so I started out with pieces from the thrift store over at the Boy's and Girl's Club."

"I don't think anyone will mind, Grace." I grinned into the mirror, holding golden straps adorned with draped blue chiffon at my shoulders. The empire waist reminded me of Jane Austen novels. "It's gorgeous."

"We'll see." She jerked her thumb at the rest of the garment bags on the collapsible rack. "When everyone else gets here to pick theirs up."

Dorian showed first. He didn't stop to open the bags he took, one for him and the other for Alex.

"I totally trust your fashion sense," he said.

Similarly, Faith picked up Hal's as well as hers. She peeked. "White? Interesting choice for him."

"All Hal's accessories are red to match yours." Grace shrugged. "I didn't want him to blend in with his chair, is all."

"This is different though." Faith held up a round hammered copper disc on a comb. "I like it." She stood at the mirror, holding it up behind her head.

Kitty took one look at the beaded yellow drop-waist dress in her bag and crowed. Eston's reaction was a sedate grin as he nodded over the silver pinstripe on navy.

"We're going to look like the Roaring Twenties." Before the door closed behind them, she added, "Thanks, Grace!"

Hailey and Bailey insisted on taking theirs out of the bag. Hailey's was sunrise mauve tulle with a tea-length circle skirt in a '50s design. Bailey's was bias-cut peach satin in a draped mermaid, like a 1940s movie star.

"Rita Hayworth hairstyle, here I come." Bailey grinned. "You owe me twenty bucks, Hale."

"Worth it." Hailey beamed. "Thanks, Grace. The boat party is a casual event. I can't believe this is the last dance with one of your creations."

"Well, I'm going directly into business." She smiled back. "State of Grace dot com if you need anything at college or other occasions."

"Wow." Bailey blinked. "You've got a whole plan."

Grace only nodded as they headed out.

"What about school, though?"

"Salem State business school for me." She smiled. "I know everyone else is looking at Ivies abroad or in Rhode Island. I want to invest in my business while getting the parchment to support it. That's not in my budget, either financially or timewise."

"I hear you." I swallowed.

Logan and Dylan knocked on the door next. So much had changed since the first time we'd done the pre-dance outfitting ritual. For the better, because all of us felt so comfortable that their presence didn't derail me.

"Guys, I'm still not sure what I'm doing after graduation."

"I kind of figured." Logan patted my shoulder. "Whatever you do, I'm in your corner."

"Well, not everyone's early acceptance like Faith or Logan here. Even I don't have that all hammered down." Dylan sighed. "Whichever school gives me the biggest scholarship is where I'll end up. I'm waiting to see what I get after the big games on the common."

"It's all too much fuss if you ask me." Grace sighed. "That the adults make, I mean. The whole idea that everyone has to be a hundred percent sure what they want to do forever. There's no wrong way, Aliyah. Only the one that works best at the time."

"Yeah." I nodded. "You all have a point. Thanks, guys."

A few nights later, it was time for the dance. Hal wasn't at the top of the stairs like last time, even though we had the same formal introductions they did at Parent's Night. Instead, Faith stood alone, behind Logan and me but ahead of everyone else. Hiram Hawkins still insisted on sticking to the oldest-fashioned interpretation of school rules. I realized that there was no way around it. He had no choice but to make an exception for Hal.

His chair sat at the foot of the stairs. He rose when we got halfway down, pacing forward slowly, as though he walked on the bottom of the ocean with leaden boots instead of across a few feet of parquet in the same atmosphere as the rest of us. Hal's grin stuck to his face like festive decals on a window. The white of his suit shone like a star. She took his hand and together, they paced behind Logan and me on the dance floor.

"By request," Dorian murmured into the mic. The music started, *Never Tear Us Apart* by INXS.

Logan gazed over my shoulder, nose and eyes reddening as tears trickled down his face.

"What's wrong?" I asked.

He shook his head, unable to answer with words. Instead, he turned us and I saw everything he had.

Hal Hawkins hadn't always felt well at our dances. I'd watched him take it easy, let Faith lead, even go so far as striking poses as she moved around him. This was almost horrifyingly different.

Although he'd grown a few inches taller than her, Hal clung to Faith, leaning his head on her shoulder as if he hadn't the strength to hold it up himself. They barely even swayed. At first, I wondered why she didn't help him back to his chair and continue dancing from there. Then I saw his lips moving.

He's singing it. To Faith.

Logan and I spent the rest of the song leaning on each other's shoulders, sniffling occasionally. At the end, Faith did lead Hal back to his chair. He moved it along to the punchbowl after Grace took her arm and led her off to dance to the next song, which was *Keep Holding On* by Avril Lavigne.

"I need a minute," Logan said.

"Me too."

We started away from the punch bowl, the reason unspoken between us, how we should compose ourselves before checking on Hal.

"Turn around, Morgenstern." Coach Pickman stepped in our way, brandishing a tiny package of tissues. Coach Chen stood beside her, nodding. "Take these if you want, but don't leave him there by himself."

I nodded, taking the tissues and Logan's hand. We went back like she said and found Hal alone and in as much need of the packaged paper as we were.

"Thanks. The napkins make my skin all chapped," he managed. "I don't blame you for trying to jet."

"We were coming back," Logan said.

"Well, then." Hal managed a grin. "Would you mind getting me some punch before anything, uh, happens to it? I'm not up to getting tipsy tonight."

I ladled out three cups and passed them around.

"Don't worry." Xan stepped out of the shadows beside the DJ table. "Your liquor's at another party."

"Did you just make a Mario joke?" Logan blinked.

"Played a lot of video games over break." He turned his hand and stared at his fingernails, which were purple to match his tie. "Don't ask me where."

"I know." I nodded. "Walls and ears."

"Alexander." Mrs. Onassis stepped up beside her son, bumping into me in the process. "Come away from the rabble and dance with your old mother." She looped her arm through his, locking it into what looked more like a martial arts grip than a friendly gesture.

"Old?" Logan shook his head.

He had a point. She looked more like a college student than a woman with a recently adult son.

"Flattery will get you everywhere." She dropped Logan a wink. Then narrowed her eyes at me of course.

"Eww." Hal waved one hand in front of his nose. "Sorry, Xan."

She turned her nose up to eleven and hustled away with our favorite frenemy.

"God, I wish all the parents were like yours, Aliyah." Logan sighed.

"Even magic wishes can't do that." Andre Gauthier reached for the punch ladle. "The only way out of such trouble is through, and breaking the patterns, Mr. Pierce."

"You know an awful lot about magic wishes, Mr. Gauthier." I dropped Logan's hand and put mine on my hips. "You ought to take your advice. Like standing up to Mrs. Onassis instead of hiding from her."

"She's beyond all hope. Abandon it, ye who enter her." He chuckled. "That's uncouth, but you're all adults despite your lack of diplomas. Speaking of which." He took a metal flask out of the pocket inside his suit jacket.

"Yeah, speaking of Noah." Logan stared at Andre's nose.

"The meeting's tomorrow night. I haven't forgotten." He tipped the flask over his cup. "I will be standing up to far more substantial foes than a frustrated piggy-bank for minor Greek nobility."

Hal pointed at the wall, then his ear.

"I have my ways of dealing with that, young Hawkins." Andre grinned. "Be patient. My end of our bargain is coming to a close." He raised his cup to us as though it were made of diamond instead of plastic and sauntered off.

Logan and Hal chatted for a few moments, discussing how an undeath magus could theoretically counter both space and mind magic. I used the time to try listening on my own. So much and so many felt and sounded familiar to me. One set of vibrations stood out as strange.

I followed them, sticking to the side of the room behind the chairs for sitting and the refreshment tables. Whoever I tracked kept ahead of me, though. How they were aware, I didn't know. Unless it was another mind magus. The idea of a stranger with my barely explored ability on campus alarmed me enough to tug Professor Hawkins' sleeve.

"Sir, I, uh, sense an unfamiliar mind here."

"Thank you for telling me, Miss Morgenstern." His brow furrowed as he pressed his hand to the wall. "Please fetch Mr. Young for me."

It was easy to find Lee. He stood by the door, gazing at it because off-campus dates hadn't been approved at all this time.

"Professor Hawkins needs you."

"Why?"

"It's a security issue."

"On my way." He headed off immediately. I kept my ears open. Moments after Lee joined the headmaster, all sense of Hiram's alarm deescalated.

Logan beckoned from the edge of the dance floor. When Dorian's voice announced this was another request, I understood he'd made it. So I went directly into his arms before I even recognized *The Only Exception* by Paramore. We danced through to the first chorus, leaning with heads on each other's shoulders. He spoke.

"You deserve so much love, Aliyah," he murmured in my ear. "Like the princess finds in a fairy tale. But—" He swallowed, hands trembling against my shoulder and back. "I'm no prince. I don't know what kind of love lives in my heart because my life's mostly been a mess. But you're the first person I ever wanted to give it to."

"I love you too." I lifted my head and pulled back so he could see my face. "My life was pretty decent, but having you in it makes it a million times better."

He nodded, eyes shining.

Everything but Logan went away after that. That focus on him was almost like wearing the ear cuffs. Not only being in tune with him but attuned to each other and that song. The feeling extended to almost all the remaining music. We paused before the final song, because Hal once again rose from his chair.

Dorian played *Disenchanted* by My Chemical Romance to close out the evening. An odd choice.

Cadence had explained The Black Parade album to me ages ago since it was one of her favorites. It was about a dying young man's journey out of his life, carried away by a terminal illness. In the track *Disenchanted*, the patient looks at his life, warts and all, accepting it before laying it to rest. The lyrics fit Hal's situation so closely I wondered whether Dorian's precognitive mother had suggested he play it.

A little over halfway through, he collapsed, seizing on the floor. Dorian cut the music as of the lyrics mentioned going away, his face white as a sheet. Faith pressed her fingers to Hal's neck and her ear to his chest.

"He's not breathing!"

I joined her on the floor as we began CPR. Nurse Smith and Charles took over a moment later, but Faith never left his side. When they put him on a gurney instead of Timmy the karkinos, I knew this was the worst he'd ever been.

Minutes later, they had him out the door to meet the Emergency Medical Extrahumans at the ambulance. Mr. Fairbanks tried to stop Faith from leaving, but she held her hand up, brandishing the new ring at him. He stepped back and let her go, looking for all the world like he'd been slapped.

Maybe we all had, with an all too brutal and mundane reality.

School rules meant the rest of us had to be in our rooms with the lights out. I'm not sure any of the third-years slept.

CHAPTER THREE

The Trouble With Andre
Andre Gauthier

The incorrigible children had me over a barrel since October, and I wasn't sure how many of them knew it. Waiting practically all winter to finally exit such a compromising position hadn't been ideal. Although once they owed me a favor, Petra's long wait would end with a well-timed wish.

"Don't get ahead of yourself, Andre."

"Make yourself scarce, Gamila." I sighed over the collection of documents supporting the new arguments on my desk. Including one bombshell endorsement certain to ruffle feathers and tip scales. "You know the risks if they see you at the meeting."

"And you know what's at stake if you wish from afar." She shook her head. "You could get Logan's help to manage her release mundanely, you know. He's her blood kin."

"I could, but I want a sure bet." I smirked to banish the threatening sting at the corners of my eyes. "Wishes are guaranteed by the Queen herself."

"What will you do if Leo gets hold of my lamp and simply undoes it all?" She tapped her foot, reminding me of the classrooms downstairs. "Or worse, Abraham. Can you not imagine the ruin he'd cause?"

The shudder racked my body before I could hide it. The lamp's powers would have revealed my feelings to her regardless. Perhaps an empath had done a turn in it. I reached for the drawer—the small one, which most of my peers might use to store writing implements.

"You didn't need that Magifinil when you were my student." She raised an eyebrow. "And you don't now."

"I do." I sighed. "I've never gotten one over on Abe without it."

"You never faced him sober before."

"I did. Once." I closed my eyes and behind them, Petra stared at me through a van window. The kind with a wire mesh between two panes of glass.

"I wish you'd stop." She gazed down at where my fingertips met the bottle. "They're killing you."

"My work's too important to drop this crutch just yet. Sorry, Professor." I winced at the slip.

Mistakes like that could doom me and by extension the only person I ever loved in the very near future. So I pressed down and turned, shook two out, thought better of it, and added a third. The bitterness as they funneled down my gullet with water matched the vast portion of my life. Dramatic? No. More of an understatement. The pills were sweeter. So why did my hand shake as I returned the bottle to its hiding place?

I swept the documents into a folder emblazoned with the school's seal, then headed to the mirror to adjust my tie so it felt less like a noose. My old teacher had a point. I had no way of directing where her lamp went once my turn as its master ended. At least my enemies didn't know I had it.

For now. Because if the Morgenstern girl figured it out, Fairbanks might extract that information from her brain during those mandatory "training" sessions. I'd thought Logan less of a risk, which was why I'd sent Gamila to him in the library. With Hal Hawkins in the hospital, my only hope now was that shady Abe would underestimate him like he'd done with Petra ages ago.

"Shady Abe." I chuckled. "There I go, an old pot name-calling a kettle."

Silence stretched like the horizon at sea. Gamila Haddad-Hawkins was many things, but dishonest wasn't one of them. It must have galled her to her core, working for Richard Hopewell. I wasn't much of a step up in the honesty department, although she'd told me my motives were worlds above his.

As I left my quarters for the meeting that would decide Noah's educational fate for the second time, I prayed that Gamila's third and final master would be a better man than I.

I approached with caution, as one should when preparing to enter a pit of vipers. That wasn't fair to Hank Thurston and Justin Glen. Yes, I handled Georgina Dunstable with care. No ordinary Sidhe is granted an honorable discharge and return to mundanity from the Faerie Queen. Circumspection notwithstanding, standing still or even moving slowly grants advantages most overlook.

So, I found myself around the corner, eavesdropping on my enemies. Unsurprisingly, they discussed the recent nuptials of Harold Hawkins and Faith Hawkins, née Fairbanks.

"Doctor Morgenstern is a Justice of the Peace," Abe said. "She had them do all the paperwork at visits for their familiars. The ceremony, too."

"The nerve!" I could practically hear Lavinia press a hand to her breastbone.

"He must already be lawyering up to have it annulled." Leo snorted. "That's what I'd do with one of mine."

"You'll have to fight Hiram and Hector both over that." Lavinia clicked her tongue. "Because he married up."

"You're wrong as usual." Abe chuckled. "He's dying, so their future's over before it begins. If she stands to inherit this school, I'll tear the papers up. Otherwise, she's a pen stroke away from being disowned."

A scent of freshly crushed apple blossoms wafted past me in

Georgina Dunstable's wake. She noticed me but said nothing as she sailed past like a float at a homecoming parade.

"Honestly, Abraham." She stood at the corner, her back to me, fully obscuring the shadows where I stood. "They're adults. Talking annulment is rich, coming from you. Her mother hadn't even started her last year here before you had that ring on her finger, and pregnant with your eldest as she graduated besides."

"I don't recall it quite as you describe," he countered in a monotone. His attempt at denial might have worked if only Justin Glen hadn't strode right past and stepped through the opening Georgina gave him.

"I remember well enough. Let's get into the meeting and on to business that pertains to this school." He sighed. "Gossiping as though we're students is the opposite of setting a good example."

"We're still missing two," Leo protested.

"Let's wait in chambers," Georgina said. "This hallway's grown crowded, and my poor old feet can't take any more abuse."

Their grumbles receded as they shuffled away. Hank Thurston stepped out from behind the column across the hall from me. He paused before following the others through the now-closed door.

"Isn't it better to change with the times than be stuck in the past?" He didn't turn his head or give any other indication he knew I was there, although his words to an otherwise empty room told another story. Mr. Thurston might have arrived and hidden before I did. Then again, he might simply have had a senior moment.

I didn't speak until I'd counted a full minute after he'd gone in. That was no issue. The answer wasn't for him.

"Because no matter how I adapt, part of me always will be."

Abe Fairbanks rose as I entered the room, a move so out of character that I almost turned around and left. If he was on to me, all was lost. But his motivation was as mundane as the man himself. Almost.

"Finally, Gauthier's arrived. Now, who moves to adjourn?"

"Not so fast." I crossed to the empty podium and set my folder on it. "I've got business to bring before you all."

"I move to dismiss." Leo Pierce yawned.

"I move we hear it." Hank Thurston leaned forward in his seat.

"Oh, come on." Lavinia Onassis rolled her eyes. "You might not have a life outside this boardroom, but I do."

"I'm intrigued." Hank's fox familiar yipped in agreement. My interpretation, at least.

"All in favor of hearing Mr. Gauthier?" Fairbanks drawled.

Three hands rose, including mine. Justin Glen gave me a lopsided grin.

"Speak then. But keep it concise. That's a good lad." Fairbanks waved his gavel as I wished I could whack him in the teeth with it. I had four years on him, Leo two, and the other trustees even more. Abe was the most junior unless you counted Lavinia, which I tried never to do. But his family traced its association with the school back farthest. Barring a Hawkins or a Morgenstern joining the board, he'd hold that gavel.

"I address the matter of nonmagi on campus. Specifically, ones who attended in good faith while they were magi, but are no longer designated as such, for whatever reason."

"You ruled against the Morgenstern boy last year." Georgina Dunstable raised an eyebrow.

"Certain details have come to light. I think I might have made a mistake." I opened my folder. "The court ruled in *Salem v. Arnold* that both the defendant Jonah and his associate Noah Morgenstern acted under duress. It's neither young man's fault the latter got turned. Messing Academy didn't penalize Mr. Arnold, which casts Hawthorn Academy in a negative light."

"Messing Academy has no clause in their bylaws banning individuals on threat registries from the student body." Fairbanks shook his head. "You cited it last time in your statement."

"It's come to my attention, however, that both Dylan Khan and Aliyah Morgenstern are now on a similar registry. The one for extramagi. Mr. Khan's been on it for over a year. They both attend with no issue."

"I beg to differ." Lavinia Onassis snorted. "She's all but poisoned my son's mind with the wrong sort of values. If he doesn't come around, I'll have to write him out of my will."

Hank Thurston let out a papery chuckle, displaying the expression that gave him his laugh lines.

"What's so funny?" Lavinia's nostrils flared.

Fairbanks tapped his gavel. "More importantly, how is it relevant?"

"Well, the idea of a poison magus getting himself poisoned for one. And someone your age with a will, but I suppose that comes with 'old name, new money' territory." Her face went an alarming shade of crimson, but he only smiled and continued as mildly as the north wind. "As to relevance, any student will tell you she's spent most of the last two years keeping her distance from him when she wasn't busy being spirit week monarch and helping us win a championship title. So, I beg to differ."

"Where was he all winter then?" Two bright red spots bloomed high on her cheeks. The force of her words filled the air between her and me with the tang of wine. So I wasn't the only one hitting a bottle, even if mine rattled instead of sloshing.

"Your son's an adult, Lavinia. His moral choices are his own now." Georgina Dunstable shook her head. "Territory every parent must navigate someday, myself included."

"This isn't a discussion of individual character, but one of risk to the student body." I cleared my throat. "I think they, along with Noah, don't pose any. They want to get through school. Mr. Morgenstern only wants to be allowed on campus so he can study for and take final exams. Provided blood is in stock and he's verified well-fed, I believe it's in the school's best interests to make accommodations. As we do for any other student with different abilities."

Leo Pierce opened his mouth, then shut it again. He wasn't a genius like my Petra or his son. But he had half a brain under that professionally styled hair.

I outlined the logistics of blood storage and gave a list of potential testing locations, including the library as Logan had suggested, plus the auditorium and Creatives room, which could be easily isolated during exam week. I even gave them a list of accommodations used at other schools for former vampire staff, part of the selection of documents in my folder.

The last of those was the true pièce de résistance—a written agreement with my argument, penned by none other than Director-General Rockport. No sane person would expect teenagers to petition their bogeyman, so I'd done it for them. A stroke of brilliance on my part, judging by the silence in the room. Not even a paper rustled.

For one brief shining moment, I dared to believe in Camelot. Or the closest one could get to it in a boardroom full of privileged, scheming well-to-do ne'er-do-wells.

Chaos usurped, but Abe Fairbanks and his gavel guillotined its reign.

"So, what's your motion then, Gauthier?" His lip curled up in a sneer, a tell as familiar as my owl, Serapis. He'd read my intent already.

"I move we allow nonmagi, enrolled in good faith as magi before a change in registered status, to complete their educations."

"All in favor?" Abe Fairbanks gestured with the gavel. Four hands rose, and I won. But he thrust his implement forward and insisted, "All opposed?"

Lavinia, Leo, and Abe raised their hands, scowling in tandem like a series of sour freight cars. I watched Abe's knuckles whiten around the gavel and just barely refrained from blurting out everything I hated about him. Beginning with all of the literal and figurative headaches his mind magic had caused me through the years. But I rose above petty and premature stone throwing. My mission didn't end here, not by a long shot.

Justin Glen applauded like he'd seen a Broadway finale on closing night. Georgina Dunstable clapped like this was the golf course. Hank Thurston added whistles and a few hoots and hollers for good measure. Leave it to a swamp Yankee to raise a little hell. If I were his age and could have gotten away with it, I might have joined.

Thurston was life goals. If I ever made it that far.

***

After the door to my quarters closed, my knees buckled. Serapis hooted while flapping madly to keep me off the floor.

"Let go, old friend." I waved him away, but he didn't heed me. We'd end up on the floor together. Wiry brown arms caught me under the shoulders, carrying with them the aroma of oranges. It was Gamila lowering me to the floor safely.

"Bucket," I managed. Serapis dropped it in front of me.

The next thing out of my mouth was far more colorful but less eloquent. A side-effect I'd dealt with for the past four years as I'd homed in on my chance to rescue Petra. After I'd done that, I could quit. Once this nausea passed, I'd finish the remnants of my promise to the children and sleep the rest of Magifinil's nasty aftermath off.

Our quarters had a sitting room with a water closet off one corner. The moment my legs cooperated, I headed there, wastebasket under my arm. After washing it and myself up, I went back to the desk and jotted a note off to Noah Morgenstern, care of his sister here on campus. A formal address, a brief statement of the new policy, and a cool but firm closing.

As a Gauthier, duty required my adherence to our traditional manners. On paper, at least. If someone intercepted it, the note was unimpeachably bland.

"Now I can drop dead." I pushed the envelope through the slot leading to the pneumatic system. All my strength left with it, dropping off my body like a cast-off dressing gown.

"What about Petra?" Gamila tapped her foot against the hardwood.

I rose. Too quickly. "Sarcasm—" My knees buckled, and I swallowed the start of her name. "Mila."

"Don't call me that." She caught me again.

"Thought I knew 'bout lamps." My face felt like rubber. "How djinn work."

"You know well enough now we're not as advertised." She got under my arm somehow.

"Hope a kid gets your lamp even if it's that Alexanax. Xandralexa." I sobbed. "You know."

"I do." A twist of her hair brushed against my cheek.

The void behind the drug yawned beneath me. I dangled from Gamila's shoulder like an empty rucksack. Before finding her lamp, I used to tumble into bed after the Magifinil wore off. Sometimes I'd miss and wake on the floor, face imprinted with the grain of whatever cheap carpet the current motel employed.

After "acquiring" the lamp via unwitting vampiric help from a certain high-security magical evidence locker, my awakenings, however rude, always occurred in a bed. Djinn had their own will to an extent. As still as I'd stood since age eighteen, as underhanded as I'd become when I overheard Hiram Hawkins mention his better half's lamp being in Rhode Island, as shipwrecked as I was in the storm of addiction and this quest, my old teacher was there.

Maybe she missed her son. Or being in the lamp, in service to a fallible queen and the man who desired her throne, had tempered her. Perhaps she was simply, at the core, kinder than I'd remembered her to be. Whatever the reason, gratitude leaked from my eyes, dropping ahead of me into the darkness of sleep.

CHAPTER FOUR

I tucked the envelope from my mail slot into my blazer pocket, totally preoccupied.

Faith and Hal hadn't been at breakfast Sunday morning after the dance or anywhere on campus the rest of that day. I'd expected them back on Monday morning, which was the usual course of events whenever Hal went to the hospital on the weekend in non-emergency situations.

However, the booth I usually shared with them and Logan stood empty. Before I could figure out whether to sit in it alone or join one of the other tables, a throat cleared behind me. I turned to see Professor Susan DeBeer. Dylan stood at her elbow, shifting his weight from one foot to the other.

"Miss Morgenstern, a moment of your time, please?"

"Uh, sure." I gestured at the booth. I'd made loads of good memories there since first year, despite all the chaos and pain. It couldn't hurt to have what might be an uncomfortable conversation someplace familiar. "Works for Bubbe anyway."

If Professor DeBeer noticed I'd made a disconnected comment, she took it in stride as she sat on one side of the booth. Dylan and I got on the bench across from her. I looked up, hoping to see Ember, but she hadn't come out of the nest since she'd laid her eggs. I'd have worried, but I sensed her contentedness through our bond. Gale always managed to get food for them both.

"Mr. Khan. Miss Morgenstern. I wanted to set things right between us. Until Hal's back, all of you from Professor Hawkins' class are with me for the morning lecture. Last year, I said some awful things about extramagi. I was wrong, and I'm sorry."

If I'd been alone, I'd have told her it wasn't a big deal. That was true for me, but not Dylan. I sensed something from him, a note of discord.

"You've had, hm." Dylan thrummed his fingers against the table. "Just over a year to speak up about it. And yeah, I get why now. It's an emergency. There's one thing important to me. How do you feel about what you said?"

She hung her head. "Like a total piece of shite." She looked up. "So where do we go from here? You're welcome in my classroom with the rest of the students in your section, but I understand if you're worried about unfair treatment. So, I've spoken to the headmaster and the Ashfords. They've agreed to let you have study hall at the library instead."

Dylan blinked. "No." He shook his head, then glanced at me. "Not for me, at least. I want to be with my classmates."

"Me too." I fought the impulse to reach across the table and take her hand, as Bubbe did for anyone sitting opposite her. "The third-years are a team. We've been through a lot and mostly made it by sticking together."

Professor DeBeer's nose reddened, along with her eyes. She sniffled, then nodded. Somehow, I understood she was thinking about her old frenemy, Professor Luciano.

Maybe she's born with it. Maybe it's mind magic.

"I'll see you both in class by the bell, then." She slid across the bench on her side of the booth, rose, and walked away more stiffly than I'd ever seen her move.

"Well, that was awkward." I sighed.

"But it had to happen." Dylan shook his head, got up, then gestured at the food line. "Wish it'd been sooner, but better late than never."

"You sound like Noah." I got up and followed him.

"Thanks."

"Wow." I chuckled. "You two spending a lot of time together?" It was the closest I'd gotten to asking whether he'd said anything about his feelings.

"Our practice and your practice, but it's all business." He paused at the hot bar to load scrambled eggs and sausages on his plate. "Or I should say, he's all business."

"Sounds about right for him." Cereal clinked into my bowl from the dispenser. "You, not so much."

"Well, it's not for lack of trying. I think he's avoiding me. Or the topic. Or both." He shrugged. "Whatever. Anyway, where do we sit?"

Before I could answer, Logan waved us over to where he sat with Grace, Kitty, and Eston. "We have lecture all together. And I'm coming with you this afternoon, Aliyah," he said.

"Yeah, DeBeer um, told us," I said. "Thanks."

"Does anyone know what happened?" Kitty asked. "With Hal, I mean. Faith never came home last night."

"No." I shook my head. "Beyond that it's his illness."

"This isn't like his other flares though," Eston pointed out. "Seizures. We're all worried about him."

"Well, Professor DeBeer said we're only joining you for the morning lecture," I replied. "Professor Hawkins is supposed to be back in the afternoon." I gasped when I remembered the mail I'd picked up earlier. "Wait. Maybe there's news."

Everyone waited as I ripped the envelope open. It wasn't from our absent friends or about them. No less important, but more personal than I'd expected.

"What's it say?" Grace leaned forward.

"It's from a trustee." I shook my head. "For Noah."

"Oh." Grace blinked. "I'd forgotten their meeting was last night."

"What's it say?"

"It pertains to a couple of us, so I'll read it." I cleared my throat. "To

Mr. Noah Morgenstern, greetings. I write to inform you that Hawthorn Academy has altered its bylaws and now allows nonmagi, enrolled in good faith as magi before a change in registered status, to complete their educations. As this decision affects your situation directly, I thought it proper to send news. Please contact the headmaster to discuss arrangements and accommodations at your earliest convenience. Regards, Andre Gauthier, Esquire."

"Wow." Dylan's mouth dropped open. "He'll be so happy."

"Why don't you take a walk off campus after Lab and deliver it to him? I'll be busy." I passed the note to him.

"Sure." He beamed.

The bell ending breakfast rang. We brought our plates to the dishwashing station and headed to lecture, which passed peacefully enough. Creatives, lunch, gym, and our hour in the library went by. Our section stood outside the lab, waiting, watching, and hoping.

The bell rang so we filed into the room without Professor Hawkins. Only Logan, Dylan, Dorian, and me.

"It's giving me the creeps." Dylan waved a hand at the front of the room.

"Yeah, major goose over grave vibes for me too." Dorian walked toward the perch Julia usually sat on, but she didn't budge from his shoulder. "What gives, lady J?"

"She doesn't like the room being so empty." Logan reached down and scooped Doris up in his arms. "Neither of them do."

"I miss Ember." I sighed.

"It's bad timing, for sure, having our critters off keeping house." Dylan shrugged. "What can we do?"

"Not much."

Someone knocked on the door, and we jumped. Before any of us could answer, it opened and revealed Georgina Dunstable.

"I'm here to audit your class."

"I'd afraid it's a bit sparse at the moment." Dorian bowed his head. "And our professor's running late."

"I'm aware." Instead of settling down in the back of the room as usual for auditing trustees, Miss Dunstable took a seat at the front although not behind the teacher's bench. "I heard you were continuing an examination of faerie artifacts, and that's my favorite subject."

"That's right." Logan nodded. "We'll have to wait for the professor. He's the one with access to the materials."

"Why not tell me what you learned last time, then?"

"Odd for a trustee." Dylan put his hand over his mouth. "Oops."

"I'll take that as a compliment, Mr. Khan, all things considered." Her pale lips turned up at the corners. "Now, what did you look at on Friday?"

Dorian rattled off a list of gnome treasures, mundane items they'd won, and brought back to the Under where they got infused with magical energy.

"The last one we saw, the gnome used as teeth." Dorian pointed at his. "Because they don't have any to begin with. They looked new and old at the same time. It was weird, and I couldn't figure out why."

"I looked that up in the library Friday night." Logan grinned. "It's gnomish time magic. They can move ahead or back, but only tiny amounts of time. It's fascinating."

"And college-level study stuff." Dylan chuckled. "Smartypants."

"What else?" Miss Dunstable asked.

"Do you mind if I draw it?" Logan stood by the magipsychic screen, hand hovering over the stylus. "There's a replica but I can't find it in the box."

"Not at all."

Logan drew an old brass oil lamp on the board. Miss Dunstable wore that slight grin the entire time, which reminded me more of *Lady with an Ermine* than the *Mona Lisa*.

"Excellent work, Mr. Pierce. Although they aren't all bronze.. Did Professor Hawkins tell you how to identify the genuine article?"

That's a leading question if I ever heard one.

"No." I shook my head. "He said they're extremely difficult to identify. Is it important for us to know?"

"Indubitably." She nodded. "I think you'd have little trouble, Miss Morgenstern. Because—"

"The lamp has a mind attached to it!" Logan dropped the stylus and waved his hands. "And she's got—"

"Exactly." Miss Dunstable put a finger over her lips, then beckoned us all closer. "One other important fact about magic lamps is this. Once a holder makes the last wish, the lamp comes unstuck in space. It's impossible for any psychic, faerie, or even a dragon to know where it is until it lands."

"What about magi?"

"It takes a rare element and an even more obscure talent amongst those to track a lamp with any degree of accuracy. Or previous mastery. But that's a moot point, because former masters are exempt from taking another round of wishes. I daresay I've got nothing else to speak of on this subject here."

"Oh." Logan put his hand to his cheek. "Wow, Miss Dunstable, that was amazing."

The rest of us nodded. Maybe the odd vibes we'd gotten on arrival had something to do with this because it seemed downright destined, like something Izzy might have read in her cards.

"Well, it looks like my class has been in good hands." Professor Hawkins walked around our little cluster, taking the long way to the business end of his lab bench.

"Your students are quite astute, Hector." She smiled. "They gave me a review of all you taught on Friday."

"Excellent." He clapped his hands, the signal for us all to get back to our benches. The guys did, but I remained.

"Professor?" I swallowed. "I'm sorry, and I don't want to waste time. But we're all worried about Hal—"

"I've got a statement from him to read before we begin."

"Thanks, Professor." I walked back to sit with Logan, hoping my knees didn't wobble too much. I reached into my bag and brought the box with the ear cuffs out, which I was supposed to wear in Lab. Professor Hawkins shook his head, and I put them back.

He pulled a piece of paper out of his jacket pocket, unfolded it, and cleared his throat.

"Hal writes, 'I miss panini and beverage roulette. Faith's badgering the nurses so they gave me the good Jell-O. I'll be back in time for dinner on Monday. Dylan, don't eat all the chicken parm. Dorian, don't drink all the root beer. Aliyah, drink a smoothie before running laps. Logan, I want more Ludovico translations so get ready. Tell Lee that Nin needs about ten playdates with Scratch. Tell Grace her blanket's way warmer than anything they've got in this hospital, and I look like a fashion god thanks to her. You all make this illness suck less than it has to. See you soon.'"

The entire room seemed to exhale, including Doris and Julia, who finally went to the familiar's area while I put my earcuffs on. For a while, all we thought about were artifacts from faerie—specifically, the feathers of the three mystical birds. One was the Alkonost, a rainbow-plumed songbird connected to the Queen. The second was the Gamayun, a gray-feathered hunter, neutral and able to act as a go-between for the monarchs in the Under and this world. Last was the Sirin, a contrary corvid in service to the King. Each feather was unique, and who could use them was extremely limited.

"You'll likely never see the Alkonost's or the Gamayun's feathers." Professor Hawkins gestured at the magipsychic screen displaying images of them in 3D. "Can any of you tell me why that is?"

"They're bonded already," I replied. "The Gamayun since before I was born, and the Alkonost more recently."

"Correct." The professor nodded. "The Sirin's feather is still somewhere in one of the worlds."

"Shouldn't the monarchs be searching for it almost constantly?" Dylan asked. "Now that they're united, I mean. It would have unbalanced power before that."

"You'd think so, Mr. Khan." Professor Hawkins nodded at Miss Dunstable. "I'm not well-versed in how the monarchs operate, but perhaps our guest can do the subject more justice than I?"

"You already gave the correct answer, Hector." She nodded. "It bears repeating. Their usage is extremely limited. The monarchs believe in patterns of coincidence, that it's impossible for the feathers to fall into the wrong hands."

The bell rang. I packed my things up, mentally steeling myself for another mind magic session with Mr. Fairbanks. I paced through the halls with Logan, wishing the whole way there that I had the Faerie Queen's faith in coincidence, that somehow I'd be in the right place at the right time. No matter how risky it seemed at the moment.

Georgina Dunstable managed it. She took her chance to drop information you've sought all year.

Now I've got to keep everything she said out of Mr. Fairbanks' head. Thanks, inside voice.

You're welcome, it sang.

I stopped before turning the corner toward the offices and faced my boyfriend.

"Logan, are you going to be safe in there?" I jerked my thumb over my shoulder.

"Don't worry." He patted his translation notebook, which he'd tucked under one arm. "Ludovico's keeping me company, but not his stuff on extramagi. He went on a tangent about merfolk. Maybe it'll cheer Cadence up at practice this weekend."

"Good idea." I nodded. "Well, let's go then."

Mr. Fairbanks was on the phone when we walked in. The smile on his face was easy, relaxed, and made me profoundly uncomfortable. He spoke to the person on the other end of the line after I put the box with my ear cuffs on his desk.

"No need for that disciplinary hearing, Hiram. She's arrived." I froze, and he chuckled. "No, I don't expect I will call again. Visit your grandson. This campus is in good hands." He hung up.

I dropped into the seat behind me as heavily as the handset on the phone's base. Behind me, the rustling sound of notebook pages shook me loose from shock's vise-grip. Anger ignited in my chest. Mr. Fairbanks had been about to set my expulsion in motion, all because I'd been less than a minute late walking through the door.

"Something wrong, Miss Morgenstern?"

"I wasn't late," I blurted.

"Ten more seconds and you would have been."

He didn't expect you to show at all. Listen and learn.

I narrowed my eyes and focused, staring at his face. I ignored everything else, even something waving on the desk near where I'd rested my hand. Paper? No. I couldn't let whatever it was distract me now. Concentration had rewards if only I could manage it.

For the first time in all our mind magic sessions, I heard something coming from his. A sing-song set of piano chords, tinny and in a minor key. Like a taunt. My anger grew, but I treated it like fire magic, using the same banishing technique as in Lab or on the Bishop's Row court but turned inward. It worked. Although I imagined something crawling over my hand.

Nice job. Go farther.

It felt unusually forceful, and direct compliments weren't usually part of its repertoire. However, I trusted my inside voice as much as any of my friends. So I kept up the work of banishing, thinking back to my first year in the lab, the day I'd banished a literal inferno. I heard something else under that music coming from Mr. Fairbanks. A sound of scattering gravel, how it flies when a bike goes out from under its rider. Knee-jerk fear and confusion. From the bogeyman trustee?

His eyes widened. Instead of rising and insisting I leave or putting on some show of feather-ruffling bravado, Mr. Fairbanks did something much worse.

He smiled. It lit his face, genuine, like a child unwrapping the biggest of his birthday gifts.

The voice spoke in its usual tone instead of the strange one from moments ago. For the first time since its arrival, I couldn't make it out.

Over-banishing with fire chilled me. Over-banishing with mind magic did something similar—a sense of being outside myself, observing this scene from an impossible vantage point. I sat straight as an arrow, back not touching the chair, eyes no longer narrowed or intense. I gazed at Mr. Fairbanks instead, as I might with a solution in Lab. Like he was an inanimate object, not a person, or even an animal, magical or otherwise. Everything in the room seemed matchstick-frail and inconsequential. Like kindling, fuel to burn. Disposable. It reminded me of something. But what?

Like Temperance with Alex last year. Except that girl only copied the father she idolized. She wasn't the genuine article, couldn't be, without mind magic. You, on the other hand... Well. He must have a motive for insisting on these sessions with you of all people.

What if I toppled like the bike I'd imagined? Lost not balance, but empathy? Connecting was easy, but caring went deeper. It was *hard*. Empathy took work. Practice. And it left me open to pain whenever someone I cared for got hurt.

Just like that, I understood. Detachment, this being above and slightly to the side of everything, felt way too comfortable.

Every extramagus stereotype I'd rebelled against, every personal truth I'd fought to affirm in my first year and struggled to keep hold of in the second, flashed before my eyes. Here I was, about to lose it all and become someone I never wanted to be, just like that.

That slight discordance coming off Mr. Fairbanks moved up and sharpened. Or maybe my frequency flattened. Either way, we began meeting in the middle.

Logan hummed, one of his habits while reading. Not just any random tune, but our song. From the dance.

It pulled me back, almost. That crawling sensation on my hand intensified.

My eyes stung, and I fought to ride the wave of emotion that surged in the heart I'd detached from. Doris leaped into my lap and lay on her side. From above and slightly to the left I watched the tip of her tail flick, sea-green eyes fixed on the desk. On my hand. I couldn't make it out from that detached vantage. I wanted to know what it was.

A familiar shriek sounded outside the door. Something familiar. *My* familiar.

Ember, who hadn't moved from her nest in months, clawed at the doorknob outside. A futile exercise for a creature without opposable thumbs.

Logan twisted the knob. Mr. Fairbanks glared at him, lip curling up as he barked out a command.

"Stop!"

"No, sir." Logan shook his head. "I won't."

"Your father will hear about this."

"Fine." He pushed the door open while glancing down and to the right.

The next moment, a skinny, stinky dragonet entangled herself in my hair. My hand touched her flank, and we connected. I connected back to myself. Then burst into tears. The insect on my hand scuttled away in a flash of metallic green and blue. I didn't have time to consider the scarab because it hurt.

People sit the wrong way and end up with a foot, hand, even an entire arm or leg falling asleep. Coming back felt like that turned up to eleven, except for brain instead of body. If that makes any sense.

Ember *peeped* and I sobbed. She needed a bath and oil for her scales, her talons trimmed and filed. Was this typical for nesting dragonets, normal as they waited for eggs to hatch? I couldn't recall, but I untangled her from my hair and cuddled her, stench and all.

"Get out." I looked up to find Mr. Fairbanks out of his seat and pointing at the door. "Find someone else to attend next time, Miss Morgenstern. Mr. Pierce is no longer welcome in my office."

I stood, Doris launching herself from my lap just in time. Logan and I left in such a hurry that I forgot the ear cuffs in their box on his desk. Doris remembered. When I turned around at the end of the hall, hellbent on walking back into the lion's den to fetch them, I saw the cat trotting after us with the box in her mouth. She dropped it at Logan's feet like it was a mouse she'd killed for him.

"Thanks." He bent to scratch her behind the ears with one hand and pick up the box with the other.

"I should thank all three of you." I wrinkled my nose. "Ember, you want a bath, girl?"

"Peep." She craned her neck, turning her head back toward her nest in the eaves of the lobby.

"Brooding box wasn't your thing, huh?" I chuckled. "I get it. I, too, am no typical nester. Go on, but I'm talking to Dorian. Maybe Julia can bring you a food basket. Thanks for the rescue." I nodded at Doris and Logan. "All three of you."

"Peep!" She rubbed her cheek against mine, then took off, winging up and away.

A moment after she entered the shadows up there, a pair of birds glided out and down. I blinked.

"Are those the Overton's pigeons?"

"Yeah." Logan nodded. "I heard Ember calling them before she got to the door. They, uh, babysat I guess."

"I'd better go thank them, and the twins too."

"Maybe wash up first." He reached toward my hair. As he withdrew his hand, something pulled. "See?"

He held a desiccated scrap of orange peel. At least, I think it came from an orange. It was a little green around the edges.

We walked to the stairs. At dinner, I asked for two slices of German chocolate cake and brought the twins their favorite dessert. Dorian said Julia would send up whatever food I brought in a basket. We sat, most of us picking at our food and watching the door.

Halfway through the meal, Hal's chair glided into the dining hall with Faith pacing slowly alongside. She looked like she hadn't slept. He seemed stretched thin, duller than Ember's scales earlier.

All the third-years got up. Once everyone else noticed, the entire room gave him the same welcome. I'm not sure who started clapping, but it wasn't important because Hal brightened up immediately.

Not for the last time, I hoped.

CHAPTER FIVE

Hal made it to my next meetings with Mr. Fairbanks, and I didn't have a repeat dissociative experience. After talking the whole thing over with Ms. Khan, I had a word for the feeling. I asked her if it meant I needed more help, maybe medication.

"It's hard to tell." She shook her head. "It's unlikely unless that starts happening more frequently."

"Could it have come from him, then? Like, maybe I picked up on something wrong with him with my magic? I mean, if Mr. Fairbanks needs help—"

"Then it's up to him to seek it." She cleared her throat. "And not a subject I'm at liberty to discuss."

"I get it."

Before leaving her office, I promised to contact her right away if I dissociated again. It was a relief to get back to the routine of school, even if I still felt like the worst wasn't over. How could it be, with what Logan and I overheard during winter break? Aside from my incident, the trustees hadn't done a thing besides approve Noah's return for exams. It was all too easy to get complacent. Faith remained vigilant.

"I don't buy it for a minute," she said in the baths Wednesday night. "They're waiting for the right moment."

"If only we had some way of knowing when that was." I winced. "Although it feels like I should have that figured out by now."

"I know mind magic doesn't work like telepathy, Aliyah." She sighed. "Sorry if that sounded like a blame game."

"It didn't."

"I know my father's tells. He knows I'm watching him." She shook her head. "He's in a holding pattern. Like he's waiting for something."

"There are three of them, working together. What if he's waiting for Leo or Lavinia to do something first?"

"Maybe it's Lavinia, then." Faith shrugged. "She's like a cat in a room full of rocking chairs."

"She's already ruining Xan's life though." I paddled my feet in the water. "Her plots are all about keeping a grip on him."

"And magisupremacy, don't forget that." Faith sighed. "I saw her in town last Sunday, at some sort of ladies-who-lunch affair at a cafe on the Wharf. Mrs. Merlini was there too, with Crow hovering around. So I went in and ordered a coffee."

"Did you hear something?"

"No, only saw them shake hands. Crow went for a walk with Xan's mom afterward." Faith grimaced. "On the way out, I saw a pamphlet they'd left on the table. Natural Order propaganda."

"I forget what they are."

"It's like a bigotry pyramid scheme. Magi on top, predatory shifters as enforcers, psychics and the other shifters rank-and-file. They favor enslaving mundanes."

"And vampires?"

"Slain."

"What about Faeries?"

"Sealed in the Under."

"Ugh."

"You think Mrs. Merlini buys it?

"I've got no idea." I shrugged. "She had Crow out and about last year, threatening business owners. The idea of either of them working with Lavinia isn't comforting."

"Hmm. What was that you heard Leo say again?" She snapped her fingers, trying to remember. "The lawyering up thing he's trying."

"Conservatorship."

She shivered although the water was warm.

"What is it?"

"That's big money talk for total control. Like what Lavinia's doing turned up to eleven. Basically, like having Logan declared a child for the rest of his life."

"How is that legal?"

"It's not, with how well Logan's doing here and that scholarship to PPC. So it sounds scary but pulling it off is a long shot. A doctor would have to declare him incompetent or a danger to himself. Or he'd have to admit it himself. How likely is Logan Pierce to have a mental breakdown?"

I got into the pool without answering because I didn't like the direction my mind went. Logan wasn't my rock. He was my ocean. Seas got tossed under the right conditions. For most of his life, his parents had used that against him. He'd grown and become more confident. Was it enough?

Faith let me have my silence during our swim. After we were in pajamas, she stopped me before opening the door to the hall. Light flashed off the band of metal on her left hand before she wrapped her arms around me.

"Sometimes there's nothing you can do," she said in my ear. "You can't see it coming or fight the battle for him. But it helps to believe, even if he's losing."

I hugged her back, understanding. She was talking about Hal, not just Logan. When she pulled away, the shoulder of my robe was damp with her tears.

We studied at the cafe the next night, sitting in pairs, flipping through flashcards Dorian had made.

"Thanks, these really help," Hal told him.

"That's major praise, coming from one of you geniuses."

"You're no slouch yourself." Hal waved a card. "I didn't think of this. You did. We'd be squinting at lists in our notebooks if it wasn't for you."

"I only made them because I need serious help studying." Dorian snorted. "You all fell for my evil plan. Muahaha!"

"Would you just take the compliment, already?" Faith chuckled. "You're almost as bad as I am with that stuff."

"Okay, fine." He held his hands up. "Thanks, then."

After the study session, I felt a lot better about using so much of my time on the extra Bishop's Row practice. Until an announcement over the PA gave me an enormous shock.

"Aliyah Morgenstern, Dylan Khan, and Hal Hawkins, report to the infirmary."

The guys went along, but before I left, I glanced through the café and counted all my friends. Nobody was missing. On the way into the lobby, I looked up at Ember's nest. She and Gale were present and accounted for too. I jogged ahead of Hal and Dylan, still unable to banish my sense of fear. Too much had gone wrong.

"Noah!" I gasped and ran down the ramp and into the waiting room.

He sat there, reading a magazine with a bunch of devices attached to his arms and head, grinning up at me.

"You should see the look on your face. Seriously."

"It's not funny." I put my hands on my hips.

"Or my fault. I'm getting the required medical tests I need before moving on campus for exams." He gestured at one of the treatment rooms. "The folks who called you are in there."

I walked in to find Doctor Klein and Stephanie Hawkins with Nurse Smith. They sat looking over an open file. One of the bedside tables held a box of lancets and band-aids. A stack of oversized index cards stood beside them.

"What's all this?"

"It's the Rapid Extrahuman Typing test I asked your help with months ago." Dr. Klein grinned. "I'm testing its efficacy, and since we did your typing with the longer form method, I hoped you'd all consent to take the RET."

"I'll take it, Grandma. I have to ask something before we start," Hal said. "Why are you here, Mom? Why do you care about identifying extrahumans now?"

"I saw that after the fact." She shrugged and sighed at the end. "My —um, the doctor sent letters. About her work, how life-or-death it is. I made so many mistakes. Ones that hurt you. I can't take them back. Maybe it's too little and too late. You're the only one who can decide that. But I want to do better going forward. Say the word, and I'll leave until you've finished here."

"Oh, Mom." Hal sniffled and held his arms out. "I forgive you."

They embraced like they hadn't seen each other for a hundred years. Or wouldn't meet again for twice as long. There wasn't a dry eye in that room.

Using the lancets and smearing blood from our fingertips along rows of marked circles on the cards felt like an afterthought. In minutes, the cards with the extrahuman typing had results. Dr. Klein did one herself, which came up black on the V for vampires. Stephanie's turned pink under D for dhampyr. We all came up purple in the spot marked M for magus. Hal's was a faint thistle, Dylan's royal, and mine nearly indigo.

"The darker the purple, the more magic in your blood at the time of testing," Dr. Klein advised. "Now, let's check element typing."

As expected, my card came up purple for solar, fire, and mind. Dylan's had air and ice. Hal's made everyone besides Dr. Klein gasp. The letter A had appeared beside the S for space magic. Dr. Klein consulted her folder.

"It looks like you've got space affinity, Hal."

"How?" He shook his head. "I don't understand. I thought magiglobular anemia prevented affinities. And anyway, I was never able to dowse or any of that affinity stuff."

"Possibly, this is a side effect of your infusions." Dr. Klein said. "The magic they give you is raw, neutral as far as elements go. So your blood processes it according to your magical potential. Because the Under gives form to our truest selves, this has been seen in other cases."

"It makes sense." Nurse Smith nodded. "Somewhere way back, a Hawkins must have had space affinity. Likely before the school existed. Because this campus couldn't have been built without mapping the space between worlds. Something only a magus with space affinity could do."

Hal asked no more questions. But we'd all heard of affinities. Logan's ability to understand critters was one example. Extra talents were well documented, even if they were fairly rare. Which might be why I saw Hal in the library later, reading a book about dowsing.

I almost asked him about it, curious what he meant to do with the knowledge or the talent if he managed to use it. But he yawned. After he checked the book out, I helped him back to the dorm instead.

Hal didn't come with us to the last off-campus practice before the Bishop's Row tournament at Salem Common, but he saw us off. In his lap sat a stack of notebooks, including one of Logan's. His translations from Ludovico's journal.

"Are you sure you don't want to take a walk with us?" Faith asked.

"I'm proofreading my final documentation for the chair. I want everything perfect when it goes to state after exams." He tapped the library book and Logan's notebook, which he must have borrowed. "And doing a little extra reading on a new topic of interest."

"Sounds cool." I nodded. Logan grinned.

Faith gave him a hug and a kiss goodbye, and we headed out. As soon as the door closed behind us, Logan tugged my sleeve.

"There's affinity stuff in there," Logan said. "He says he needs to learn it fast."

"Bet he has a plan for it, then."

"I'm sure we'll see. He didn't want to talk about it on campus."

As we walked down the street, I shook my head, the ghost of a smile haunting my lips. We'd all come a long way on this journey through high school. At one point, I'd imagined we'd stop learning and set aside picking up new knowledge to review for finals.

However, learning had transformed from something we had to do into an essential part of life as magi. One that would continue long after graduation.

Practice proceeded in the usual way, with Lynn studying way up in the bleachers. Bobby had a second watcher with him this time. A man, younger than Hank Thurston but older than Andre Gauthier. He wore a purple knit cap on a head that might otherwise be bald. Bushy gray eyebrows matched a goatee that framed a lopsided grin.

The two of them sat through our entire practice and watched most of it. The newcomer seemed to doze off a few times. On one of our breaks, I stood on the sidelines peering at him while scratching my head.

"You know what he's doing, right?" Izzy held a cup of water out to me.

"Thanks." I gulped some down. "No, I don't."

"Projection."

"So he's foretelling our plays?"

"No. The out of body kind."

"Oh." My mind drew blanks. Cadence trotted over.

"Hey, what's Nate Watkins doing here?"

"I don't know." I shrugged. "Is he important or something?"

"He's a pretty big deal at Providence Paranormal College."

"Maybe he's visiting Bobby then." I shrugged. "He graduated from there."

"Doesn't explain why he's projecting during our practice, though." Izzy shook her head.

"Want me to go ask, Iz?" I patted her shoulder. "Is it like a bad vibe or something?"

"No. Nothing bad. Just curiosity and my cards are in the locker room."

"Okay."

Break ended and we finished our practice. I meant to go over and introduce myself after stowing all the equipment, but by the time we'd done that, Mr. Watkins was gone. Most of the others went home or to their respective campuses. Cadence, Izzy, and I stayed out. We ordered pizza to go at Engine House. While waiting, Izzy pulled cards and said we'd hear more about Mr. Watkins soon. We headed back to Noah's apartment, where he, Elanor, Brianna, and Arick sat playing Mario Kart.

Dylan sat on a stool nearby, strumming his guitar, not even stopping for lunch like the rest of us. I raised an eyebrow at him, but he shook his head. Noah got a mug of blood from the fridge and hovered nearby as we wolfed down delicious pizza. We chatted about the upcoming tournament next week and the big party and dance afterward.

"I can't believe they had enough in the budget to charter a harbor cruise!" Cadence glanced at Arick, who blushed. "It'll be so much fun."

"Are you going to make it, Noah?" Brianna asked. "Elanor already has permission to go as my date."

"I know." He sighed and shook his head. "I'm technically a student at Hawthorn for cram and exam the week after, but not allowed until then on my own. So the headmaster said I need an escort for the cruise."

"I'll do it." Dylan plucked a string and busied himself with tuning it. "If you haven't already got someone that is."

Noah blinked. He glanced at me, and at first, I didn't understand why.

He wants permission.

Finally, it all made sense why Noah had given Dylan the cold shoulder for so long. He didn't want to hurt me. Although he knew I'd meshed with Logan, my brother understood that our relationship wasn't exactly conventional.

So I nodded, smiled, then jerked my thumb at Dylan, who still avoided looking at anyone or anything in the room besides his guitar. Noah crossed the room in three long strides.

"I'd be honored to have your company, Dylan Khan." He smiled down. "Thank you."

I glanced up, wishing Ember and Gale were there to peep and crow about it. Lotan made up for it by swaying happily on Noah's shoulder. Izzy pulled a card out of her bag and shook her head. Before I could ask about it, my phone beeped. I took one look at the message and groaned at my mistake.

"Gotta go, guys." I tucked the phone away and headed for the door. "I'm late to go over the practice recordings with Xan."

I left in a chorus of "see you later."

CHAPTER SIX

The next week passed less eventfully than the one before. Even with an enormous game ahead, one where there'd be scouts from colleges and universities all over the world, I felt oddly calm. As I sat in the café that Friday night, I realized I wasn't alone.

"This is like being in the eye of a storm." Lee wrapped his hands around his mug of cocoa. "Resting, waiting for the wind to pick us up again, and no idea where we'll land when it's over."

"Wow, that's poetry." I intended to chuckle but it came out almost like a sob.

"You don't know where you're going either?" He blinked.

"Not a clue." I sighed. "No offers from any schools. Maybe I'll end up in the Coast Guard like my great uncle."

"I hadn't thought of enlisting." Lee leaned his cheek on his hand. "Visa might be a problem."

"You want to stay here?" I stirred my tea. "I always imagined you going to university in Europe or something."

"If I can't stay here, I'd rather go home." He sighed. "My parents worked so hard to give me a way out. They say there's no future for a magus in rural China, but the only other place that feels like home is with Izzy."

"She's in at Providence Paranormal."

"I know, like Logan. And I'm not, like you."

"Your only chance is getting scouted at the game, huh?"

"Pretty much."

"Save a seat on the college rejection ship." Dorian sat with a green smoothie, Julia perched sleepily on his shoulder. "The drawer in my desk is stuffed full of letters that say no. Coast-to-coast tour, even."

"Ditto. Let's ask Grace to make us a commemorative quilt out of those papers."

"Sorry, I burned mine." I held my hand out, palm up, and conjured a tiny flame. "Accidentally on purpose."

We laughed because the alternative was worse. Maybe that storm Lee mentioned earlier would wash something better ashore.

The next day, I couldn't eat. However, playing on an empty stomach with my history of collapsing was madness. I got a coconut smoothie with the works from the café and took it back to my room. After drinking it, I put my uniform on. The common had a tent, wards, and special transport to shield Messing's vampire players from the sun, but nowhere for us to change clothes. I had some time to think over strategy alone since Grace was still downstairs at the dining hall.

It wouldn't matter which team won. Winning boosted prospects in most mundane sports, but Bishop's Row at the college level was so new, the scouts simply wanted to see us play. So, I'd planned every-thing around showcasing the players I thought needed to be seen. Until last night, I hadn't known Lee's situation.

Grace and Lena were so solid together on defense. If I sat either of them, we might lose too quickly to show off. That left Faith or me at mid. Faith already agreed to sit for Xan against Gallows Hill since strategically we'd need her against Messing's vampire players. Showing off his poison against shifters and changelings was his best shot at getting scouted.

If Lee didn't get a student visa, he'd have to leave the country. I had a place to go no matter what. I'd step out for him in that second match since his conjuring speed made up for my dual magics.

That's settled. Don't be tardy now.

I headed out onto Essex Street, ending up in a throng of students, staff, and faculty. Everyone, not only the Bishop's Row team and the cheer squad, was coming. Even the trustees, although Andre Gauthier looked green around the gills. I searched the crowd for one face in particular because I wanted to run my strategy for sitting out by Hal. I didn't find him.

The pit of my stomach dropped until I asked Faith where he was.

"He's watching on an orb with his dad. Saving his spoons for the boat cruise."

"At least he can still see you play." I told her my idea, along with why I was changing the rotation.

"You're something else. You know that?" She grinned.

"Did I hear you right?" Grace tapped my shoulder. "You're benching yourself against the hard-mode team?"

I nodded. "Keep it quiet. I want to tell the rest of the team together."

"That's our captain." Grace smiled.

After I attached my ear cuffs and we'd put on our ballistae, ankyr, and cestus, we huddled up. Dylan nodded, Xan blinked, and Lee cheered. We broke, and I ran out on the field, leaving Lee and Xan on the sidelines.

The game against Messing went better than I'd hoped. They had two vampire girls from first and second year in addition to Jonah, and their conjures were fast instead of powerful. Grace and Lena both had enough brute force to absorb their throws easily and Faith tagged them out pretty quickly. They didn't have Jonah's power, and Faith's orbs were too hefty for them to block.

Izzy was our most formidable opponent. She managed to tag me and duck behind Jonah in time to evade Dylan's massive ice orb. She'd surpassed me for sure. She got Lena too, although Jonah went down right after that under Grace's umbral throw. Grace's cestus flashed red a moment later. I stood at the side, watching with a furrowed brow. That tag came from out of nowhere. Grace didn't call time out, only grumbled as she stepped beside me.

Izzy was somehow the last Messing player standing, but only three of her teammates stood aside when there should have been four. It confused me so I counted again while scratching my head.

"Watch out!" Grace shouted to Faith. Finally, I noticed that other player. A guy I'd never seen before. "Umbral affinity three o'clock!"

Of course, Izzy's secret weapon couldn't possibly have umbral affinity. That was a magus thing. Telepaths sometimes had a similar trait. Just like that, he tagged Faith out. Dylan stood alone, staring at the telepath player because if you looked away from folks with powers like that, you'd never remember they were there in the first place.

Dylan dual conjured, a trick he'd only worked on at the gym on campus. He wasn't amazing at it but shocked both Izzy and the telepath with the play. He almost hit himself in the face with his air orb but managed to launch it along with the ice one. The telepath tried jumping in front of Izzy to absorb both tags, but he went down under the ice, leaving the air orb in play.

Dylan's air orbs dissipated slightly under normal conditions, increasing in diameter. With a dual conjure, they doubled in size.

Izzy hit the dirt too late. We won. Barely.

In the middle of the court, we took turns shaking hands with our opponents.

"Good game." Izzy smiled.

"Good game," I replied.

Dad and Bubbe came down from the bleachers to say hello.

"Nice strategy, kid," Dad said.

"We wouldn't have squeaked out that win if Grace hadn't seen their telepath."

"You're the one who put her on defense." Dad shrugged. "I've got dad-tinted glasses on." He grinned at the others. "Amazing work, everybody. You would have given my old team a run for their money."

"You were a team captain, Mr. Morgenstern?" Dylan blinked.

"Yeah, I was." He smiled. "Runs in the family I guess, because Bubbe was too."

"Why didn't you ever tell me?" I chuckled at my grandmother.

"Back in those days, Hawthorn was much bigger, with four divisions in each year. It's why you see things like Root or Berry on the older trophies." She shook her head but still grinned. "Mine was Branch, and you won't see that because we lost every match but had a blast."

After they left, we watched the Messing cheer squad's interpretation of *Natural* by Imagine Dragons. Their act was solid although once again unconventional for a cheer routine.

"Looks more like something that belongs in a Broadway musical finale," Dorian commented from his seat behind the sound equipment. "Probably on purpose." He pointed out a woman in the front row on the opposite side of the court. "She's the NYU faculty member who signed my rejection letter. Bet Jacinda gets in."

"Did you hear back since early acceptance, though?" Dylan asked. Dorian shook his head. "Don't give up hope then, mate. You're still in for regular."

Our team's break continued through the match between Messing and Gallows Hill.

"Ouch!" Lee winced as Jonah ended up on his back under one of Crow's orbs. "When did Merlini get so brutal?"

"I don't know. He never came to weekend practice." I shrugged. "Brianna says he's their MVP now."

"And you want me off reserves?"

"Well, you and Xan. Yeah."

He whistled. "You sure you still want to put me out there? I think you're the only one with the firepower to counter him."

"Absolutely." I grinned. "Don't underestimate yourself. You conjure faster than anyone else on our team, and most of theirs."

Izzy was the last woman standing and turned sideways to make a smaller target, panting as she struggled to gather enough energy for one more orb. Even the dodgy telepath got tagged out. Brianna still had Azrael on defense and Crow at mid. All three of them threw, and that was the end of Izzy's last stand. Gallows Hill won.

"I'm nervous." Lee wrung his hands.

"We all are." Dylan grimaced.

"Not me." Grace smiled.

"Good." I patted her back. "That's the kind of defense we need. Right, Lena?"

She nodded and cracked her knuckles while grinning like a wolf at Crow Merlini, who'd left the court without a single handshake for his opponents.

"What are you doing?" Xan asked.

"Getting ready to make bully toast," she murmured.

"Gods, I'm glad you're on our side." Xan let out a nervous chuckle.

"Relax." Dorian waved a hand. "Cheer time part two."

Cadence led her squad out on to the field. Dorian waited for her nod, then pressed a button. I sat there blinking, totally stunned. I shouldn't have been. Because, like at the talent show last year, Cadence used music as a weapon. This time was pop instead of punk, a dance remix of Taylor Swift's *We Are Never Ever Getting Back Together*.

Almost everyone over on the Hawthorn side cheered, and a few laughed. But not Grace.

"What?" I asked her.

"Trouble." She jerked her chin at the Gallows Hill section. "He's nothing nice, but you already know that. Acts like she's like his property or something."

Crow sat with his jaw clenched, fists too. I didn't like how his eyes glittered. They reminded me too much of Halloween when he almost attacked Hal and me. I glanced at Messing's benches, where Izzy sat staring down at something in her hand. A card. She paled.

I had no time to go over and ask her about it because once Gallows Hill's routine ended, I had to send my team out on the court for the final match of the day.

It went better than I expected after watching Messing's defeat. We lasted longer than them by a full three minutes, mostly thanks to Lee's near constant barrage of wood orbs. Lena absorbed three of Crow's uber throws by holding the most compact conjures I'd ever seen. Also, her stature and slight build made her a difficult target.

Grace took a direct hit from Brianna to save Dylan. Lee managed to bring Azrael down by tossing on the right after Lena discarded an absorbed orb to Az's left. Xan stepped up, running between the mid and defensive lines to misdirect and block, employing one of my plays from the videos.

Brianna took Xan down right after that. If she'd been used to seeing him on weekends, she might have done it sooner, but I think she underestimated him. Lena howled for all the world like a wolf shifter and threw at Brianna. She would have won us the game right then and there, but Bar took the hit for his captain and Crow followed up while Lena was vulnerable and tagged her out. She'd gotten over-confident.

It was going rough out there. Dylan started his double conjure, but Crow knocked the air orb right out of his left hand. Lee went into a sort of overdrive at that point, forcing Crow to defend himself. As they duked it out and tagged each other simultaneously, Brianna tossed a solid glamour ball at Dylan, whose ice orb was only half-formed. Direct hit. Game over.

Everybody cheered because the plays were brilliant on both sides. Gallows Hill's section of bleachers went wild. I headed out on to the court with Faith to join the line of players. I grinned at my team.

"You all rocked it out there, and I'm so proud. Thanks for being the best team ever. Hope you're not sore that we lost this one."

"Nah." Dylan grinned. "Everyone we played with today was a friend."

"Almost." Grace rolled her eyes in Crow's general direction. He'd walked right past us without stopping to shake hands.

"One bad apple." Lee shrugged.

"He'd better not spoil a single one of that bunch." Faith jerked a thumb at Bar and Az, who marched off the court with Brianna on their shoulders.

As I thought about leading my team back to our seats, Logan approached, walking a ways ahead of his squad.

"Sorry, Aliyah." He hugged me.

"It's cool." I hugged back. "You've got a routine to lead. Knock it out of the park, Logan."

"Thanks."

The players left to make room for our other classmates to show off. We weren't disappointed. Hawthorn might have lost the tournament, but we won the cheer competition. They did a practically flawless performance to *My Songs Know What You Did In The Dark* by Fallout Boy that used every participant's magic. The familiars joined in, too.

The Overtons danced like dervishes, extending their leaps into near flight with air magic, framed by their pigeons. Logan and Eston made rainbows with fine sprays of mist backlit by lights their familiars carried. Every time the lyrics mentioned fire, Kitty shot jets of it from both hands, boosted above the rainbows by Arick.

The entire crowd got on their feet, swaying in the stands.

Except for Leo Pierce. He sat sour-faced, as though his son, the routine, or even the song itself gave him personal insult. Maybe it did. Noah played that song on repeat for practically six months so I happened to know it was pretty scathing. Especially to a fire magus with tons of skeletons in his closet, like Mr. Pierce.

At the end, I removed my ballistae, ankyr, and cestus. Also my ear cuffs. I looked up to see Bobby Tremain grinning at me from across the field, both thumbs up. He pointed at another man hurrying across the field toward my team and me. Mr. Watkins. I nodded and smiled back. Before he got there, something else happened.

"Khan, is it?" A voice with an across-the-pond accent sounded behind me, much more polished than Dylan's. I turned to see a nimble-looking fellow with gray at the temples of his otherwise sandy hair. He extended his hand. "Coach Nigel Quinn. From Oxford Occult."

"Yes, sir." Dylan nodded and took it. "You played for the London Ravens. MVP five years in a row."

"Indubitably." He nodded. "You're a brilliant player, but I'm sure you're already aware. I'd very much like you on my junior team, if you haven't made a decision yet on a university, that is."

"I haven't, sir."

"We're covering tuition for our players although not room, board, books, or fees. If that's feasible for you, please do consider my offer, Mr. Khan."

"I'll talk it over with me mum. I mean, I'll discuss it with my mother, sir. Thank you, sir."

"Very good." He produced a card from his coat pocket. "Please contact me with your decision, one way or another. Good day."

He sauntered away, not across the field as I expected, but into the bleachers behind us. I turned to see who he approached, but before that happened, someone cleared their throat behind me.

"Bobby Tremain called me a million times about you and your team. Lynn, too. Said I'd have to see it to believe it."

My mouth dropped open. Had they been scouting me all that time? I remembered where I'd heard of him before.

"Um, see what? Sir."

Nate Watkins was the toughest professor at PPC. Not just academically, either. He'd endured a magical coma, out of his body for months, harmed by bad old Uncle Richard. Now here he was, dangling a future I hadn't realized I still wanted over my head.

"You're the captain here, Morgenstern." Mr. Watkins raised an eyebrow. "But you barely played. Tell me, why is that?"

Was this a test? A million different answers flew around my brain. Strategy, synergy, following classic plays from the game's history. None of those impressive-sounding answers was the truth.

Go with honesty, then.

"I wanted to give them all a chance to play because they deserved to be seen." I glanced at Xan. "They're all my friends."

"You applied at Providence Paranormal College back in September." He glanced down at his phone and frowned. "Early acceptance denied, I see."

"Yes, sir."

"Hey, you." He snapped his fingers. "Team Hawthorn. Tell me what you think of Morgenstern here. Would you play on a team for her again?"

"Definitely." Faith nodded.

"Three more years and then some." Grace smiled.

"Any time." Lee grinned.

"Yup," Lena mumbled.

I looked down at my shoes, waiting to see whether Xan would snark off about me or follow the crowd with hollow platitudes. He did neither.

"She never gives up and doesn't hang anyone out to dry. Not even me."

"What's that mean?" Mr. Watkins glanced at his jersey to check his name. "Onassis?"

"It means I was a total douche canoe for a year and a half." He cleared his throat. "She could have sat me all day here. Instead, she recorded practices I couldn't make because I work and put me in against our toughest challenger. Sir."

I looked up. Xan's face was red. Mr. Watkins chuckled, then peered down at his phone and shook his head.

"Well, you've still got another year to go at Hawthorn, Onassis, like Zanelli. Plus, I promised Nigel I wouldn't try poaching Khan. Anyway, I'm putting together the first official junior team for PPC, and I want the rest of you on it. Mendez, Collins, and Micello already said yes. Practice starts the same week as orientation."

"But we're not accepted." Lee blinked.

"Yeah." I nodded. "I even got a rejection."

"Early acceptance doesn't mean no acceptance, kiddos." Mr. Watkins chuckled. "Your letters are in the mail Monday morning."

"*If* they play." Xan crossed his arms over his chest. "That's what you mean, right? This is an ultimatum, some kind of *quid pro quo*?"

"No." He shook his head. "That happens to be when this batch goes out. There's scholarship money for anyone on this team from a former student's memorial trust."

He looked tired for a moment. I knew all too well what that look felt like. I wanted to say yes more than anything, but he hadn't come to recruit me. He said he wanted a team, including my friends in need.

"What do you say, folks?"

"Are you all mad?" Dylan blinked. "Don't you want something big to celebrate at the party tonight? Take the offer!"

He got his drafts, minus one. Grace declined, as I expected. That didn't faze Mr. Watkins.

"Yeah, Ambersmith gave me the same answer. Nigel also took Merlini." He shrugged. "Having a little room on the team is a good thing. Tryouts hype everyone up."

Noah stood with Elanor, giving me his best golf clap. Between his first and middle fingers, I saw a duplicate of the card Nigel had given to Dylan. Was Oxford Occult looking at him too? I couldn't ask until later, because he got into an enclosed transport with the students from Messing.

Finally, I knew what I'd be doing for the next four years. With my friends.

Most of them, anyway.

CHAPTER SEVEN

The boat cruise was a casual affair, so Grace hadn't made outfits for it. In a way, that was a relief. I'd have felt overdressed in a major way, wearing Hawthorn formal with everyone else in t-shirts. The boat didn't leave until eight, so we all had dinner before going upstairs to get ready. That was a good thing since my appetite returned with a vengeance on the way back to campus from the games.

Logan still showed up at my door wearing a sea green tie with a blue shirt and navy sport coat. His eyes sparkled like light on the ocean. I smiled because he looked happy and at ease like a weight was off his shoulders. I wasn't sure why, so I asked.

"It's hard to explain." He shook his head. "I wouldn't have thought so if you'd asked me yesterday. It's because I won a performance competition, one with critters involved. But, I did it on my terms, without anyone or their familiars feeling uncomfortable. I think that's why he wasn't happy about it."

"You took something you were raised to do and made your way with it." I nodded. "I'm proud of you."

"He's not." Logan sighed. "No matter what I do or how well it turns out, he's never satisfied. Maybe that's not as important as I thought it was. Your mom came right over after the routine. She said I exceed expectations. Maybe that sounds a little odd to most people. Not me."

"That's how Mom talks sometimes. She's right because you do." I took his hand. "If your father can't see it, that's his loss."

We headed down the stairs and off-campus, this time in a group of all the third-years, and their plus ones..

Hal's chair glided easily along Essex Street and to the Wharf, where we got on the boat. The festivities took place on a three-season deck with a solid roof overhead with columns evenly spaced along it for extra support. In foul weather, the sides would have had windows and panels up. Since it was balmy, only the windows stayed up, giving us a partially outdoor venue.

Messing was already there, and Gallows Hill arrived after we had. I looked around for Izzy, but Lee had found her first. I let them have some time together, figuring he'd want to tell her the good news about college.

Cadence squealed and dashed in my direction. I braced for impact unnecessarily since she ran right past me and embraced Arick. Romantically—I'm talking like hands in the hair and open-mouth kissing. Logan and I stood there blinking while Xan chuckled and Dorian applauded.

"Whoa." Eston reached into his pocket. "Guess I owe you twenty bucks, Dorian."

"Should have talked to Dylan before making that bet." Xan grinned. "He's known about Carick for a week straight."

"Wouldn't that be Ardence?" Eston raised an eyebrow.

"They liked Carick better."

I glanced at a stack of audio equipment, waiting to see what kind of entertainment they had planned. If it were Piercing Whispers, Dylan wouldn't have gotten the chance to ask Noah on that date. After a moment, I saw a familiar face.

"Hey, is that—"

"Uncle Paolo, yeah." Bar leaned against a nearby column. "He's a landlord, but karaoke's his real job."

"Did you say karaoke?" Dorian waved Eston's money away. "Keep that yuppie food stamp for refreshments later. I'm glad those two are at the PDA stage. Well, this just became the best party ever."

"Thanks." Eston smiled and put the bill back in his pocket. "Want to go look at that list?"

They headed off toward some tables, where Paolo had left a stack of notebooks with his selection of songs. I intended to go with them.

A sudden high-pitched whine made me wince. At first, I thought it came from Paolo Micello's equipment, but he stood holding the cord, about to plug it all in. Nobody else reacted, and it had sounded behind me. I turned.

Crow leaned against the boat's railing outside the nearest window. He had one hand in his pocket, and the other made a fist in front of his chest. With eyes narrowed and upper lip curled, he turned his back on Cadence and Arick as they chattered over the available karaoke songs. I lifted a foot, about to go over and check on him.

Don't even think about it.

I watched him stalk toward the gate, where we'd all come up the gangway. We'd already embarked so it was closed. The ramp lifted minutes ago. Instead of hanging his head or dropping his shoulders, Crow continued walking between the railing and the windows. I hoped he'd maybe find someplace private to shift and fly home. "Don't think that's happening."

"Nothing good can come from that, yeah?" Dylan said.

He and Noah stood at my shoulder. I turned while sighing.

"Best I can imagine is he goes home."

"No." Noah shook his head. "He's got some scary older siblings. Home for him means coming back with reinforcements."

"Mavis seems like a good kid, though." I raised an eyebrow.

"She's the odd duck in that house, like the apple that rolled into another orchard." Noah wrinkled his nose. "I'll hope he goes anywhere else in town besides there."

As it turned out, he did neither thing.

We'd earned that celebration, but it felt as temporary as finishing a collaborative chalk mural with thunderclouds on the horizon. Bright colors were everywhere, as were the flash of phone cameras and a sense of flying time. Almost all the students sang, except for Kitty who said she'd sound better wearing tinfoil gloves and scratching chalkboards, and Crow stuck to one of the two corners. Everybody danced when we weren't singing. Alone, in groups, and with each other. Even the faculty, staff, and trustees.

The dance floor was packed while Grace sang *Boombayah* by Blackpink. When she finished, and Noah got up to sing *Impossible Year* by Panic! At The Disco, even the friends dancing in groups stuck around. Some of them lit up their phones and waved them in the air.

Toward the end of that song, Lavinia Onassis tried to drag Xan out on the dance floor with her. Dorian grinned and stepped between them.

"Allow me, milord." He gave Xan's mother a borderline absurd theatrical flourishing bow. "Milady, if I may?"

At first, Lavinia simpered, smiling as he led her away to the dance floor. Behind her back, Dorian gave the next singer a wink. It was Cadence.

"What's she singing?" I asked Arick.

"She only told us it's from the '90s and called *Bitch*. Mrs. Onassis isn't going to like this." He winced. "Dorian knew that going in."

"I'm never letting him call himself a coward ever again." Dylan shook his head.

"Brass balls." Noah nodded sagely. "He has them."

Cadence nailed the song, singing directly at Crow, who fumed even more over by the refreshment table. His grip shattered the clear plastic cup in his hand. He dropped it, then blended into the crowd. Dorian jounced Lavinia around the dance floor, pointing at her every time the song's title came up with his goofiest grin. The best and worst thing happened.

Everybody laughed.

The sound coming off the crowd was pure release because the Hawthorn students mostly feared the trustees and our friends at the other schools knew how we felt. Our coaches and professors must have joined in for a different reason. I couldn't imagine what that was, but it felt like they meant to laugh with her. But the trustees laughed *at* Lavinia Onassis.

She didn't realize this until the song was half over, at which point she stomped off toward the ladies room, glaring at me the entire way, for some reason.

"I don't get it." I shrugged.

"You will." A low, intense voice sounded behind me.

I turned and found only Lena there.

"Did you say something?"

She shook her head. Her presence confused me for a moment. Only third years and their dates were supposed to be at this party. Dylan had brought Noah, Cadence brought Arick, and Dorian invited Xan. Who'd brought Lena?

Bar sauntered over with a bottle of water and handed it to her.

"Thanks, Bartholomew." Her voice came out a little raspy, definitely not the same as whoever had spoken before.

"Next time we face off on the court, breathe from the gut before howling." He grinned down at her.

"Not gonna say I shouldn't?" She blinked.

"No way, short, small, and ferocious." He shook his head. "Just advice. Uncle Paolo says breathing right helps save your pipes."

She put the water down. "Let's dance." They headed off and did exactly that.

Logan linked his arm through mine and raised his eyebrows. I nodded, and we followed them. Izzy was up at the mic with Lee, singing *You're My Best Friend* by Queen. For those few minutes, I forgot about all the drama and that mysterious voice, at least until the next singer got up.

Crow chose a song on the radio from back when Bubbe was our age, one a lot of people considered plaintive or even sweet. My grandmother had assured me that *Every Breath You Take* was nothing nice no matter how pretty the music sounded. People kept right on dancing, too. Logan grimaced at the lyrics and gladly sat out the rest of it with me. We found Cadence and Arick by the refreshment table, and both were put off.

"It's been six months already." Cadence wrinkled her nose.

"Yeah, what gives?" Logan shook his head.

"Be careful." I patted Cadence's arm. "He's dangerous."

"I should say the same thing to you." She gave me a half-grin. "With the way that trustee woman's been glaring at you all evening."

"She thinks Aliyah messed with Xan's mind," Logan said.

"Well, you've been a good influence on him." Arick nodded. "Which she doesn't like."

"Huh?" Logan blinked along with me because Arick didn't know what we'd overheard on winter break.

"She's been stopping by at our room all year, asking to be let in." He shrugged. "Xan always says no because he doesn't want her there. She blames Aliyah for that. So yeah, you've got something there, Logan."

"Why do parents suck so much?" Cadence sighed.

We all looked across the room, where Professor Hawkins and his ex-wife stood together in what could only be an awkward conversation. How she managed to keep her position as principal at Gallows Hill after pretending to be psychic, I didn't know. It wouldn't have flown at Hawthorn, but Gallows Hill didn't have trustees controlling everything.

Lavinia Onassis sat in a corner, nursing a bright blue cocktail. She wasn't alone in it anymore, however. Crow sat listening to her and shaking his head. She handed him something I couldn't see. I almost followed him to investigate. When he went to the bar and returned with a water, I figured it was only money and let it be.

That turned out to be a mistake.

The music changed as Paolo performed *All Star* by Smashmouth. We all got back out on the dance floor. After that, Azrael sang *Yellow Submarine* by the Beatles. Lena surprised us all with a rendition of *Volare* in Italian.

After that, Paolo set up a playlist and took a break from the karaoke for a bit.

Dylan, Elanor, and Noah chatted over one of the books while

selecting a song. Izzy stood across the room separated from me by the crowd, waving a tarot card. I couldn't hear her over the music, but she held The World reversed. Cadence's card. Not good.

The exact opposite of good, in fact.

I wasn't sure where Cadence had gone. Crow was nowhere to be seen.

My ears practically stung with discordance. Since that always seemed to mean trouble, I followed the sound past the half-open enclosure, out toward the railing on the starboard side. Halfway down from the prow I found trouble.

Cadence faced Crow with her hands on her hips, back pressed against whitewashed steel tubes, the only thing separating her from the depths of the harbor. Which we were at the edge of, judging by the tankers on the horizon's edge.

A soft hiss came from my left. I turned my head to see Logan with Doris on his shoulder, her tail up and bushed out.

"You're taking me back." Crow's voice sounded hollow, as though he read from an encyclopedia, stating facts. "Then coming to Oxford with me. End of discussion, Cadence."

"Crow." She rolled her eyes. "We're not even friends anymore."

"You'll do what I say." He reached out and grabbed her wrists before she could pull away. "Because you're mine. Forever."

"Let her go." Arick stood on the other side of them with his hands conjuring. His wood magic was there but faded somehow.

"Get lost, kid." Crow tilted his head. "A man's talking."

"Being an asshole doesn't make you a man." Arick's hands shook, and his voice cracked. But he threw.

Or at least tried. The orb fizzled out the moment it left his hands.

Crow laughed, then took one hand off Cadence and made a fist.

"Stop!" I knew that tone in Cadence's voice, but the command in it fell flat.

Arick raised his hands, holding another orb to absorb the blow. This one fizzled too, and he took the hit on the chin. He fell to the deck, knocked out. Skinner crawled out of his jacket and crooned on his chest.

Cadence opened her mouth and drew a breath, about to scream. He opened his fist and placed his palm over it.

"It's me or the ocean, bitch." Crow leaned forward, catching my friend between him and the rail. "The Boss knows about the DelMar exile. There's a new order coming to town. The only way you and your folks get to stay on land is you with me. Choose wisely." He took his hand off her mouth and tapped his foot, waiting for an answer.

"Wow." Cadence blinked. "You can't even call her your mom anymore? How pathetic."

Crow slapped her. Doris hissed.

I moved to defend my friend although magic wasn't working the way it should. Logan held my hand in a vise grip and shook his head while pointing at Arick.

"Don't, Aliyah," he breathed. "You can't win without magic."

"I can." Xan stepped out of the shadows, near where Arick still lay knocked out. "Don't make me hurt you, Merlini."

"Queers like you can't fight." Crow snorted.

Xan chuckled. "You're a shittier bully than I ever was. Let her go."

"This ain't your business."

"I've been where you are, Crow. Someday, you'll wish you never did this." Xan shook his head. "So let her go."

"Make me." Crow leered. "Your mom said you're due for a thrashing."

Xan swung at Crow, fist arcing through the air on a collision course with his face. He dodged it but had to release Cadence in the process. Enraged, Crow let out a sharp cry. A knife gleamed in his hand, not the one from the park months ago.

For some reason, it reminded me of my ear cuffs.

He slashed, and Xan ducked. Instead of a slice across the face, a lock of black hair blew away in the breeze. I waited for Xan to swing again, or maybe conjure poison and throw an orb Bishop's Row-style. He didn't. Instead, he waited.

The next time Crow slashed, Xan blocked with a kick. This time, the end of a shoelace went flying.

I beckoned to Cadence, trying to coax her away from the railing.

She stood like a statue, eyes fixed on the fight. If I'd had Ember with me, I would have sent her over. She was back at school, nesting. So I tried mind magic to get Cadence's attention.

Easier said than done. For whatever reason, I couldn't catch her gaze, no matter how much I focused on her. It wasn't going well for my former enemy, either.

"Get help," Xan panted.

Blood dripped off the side of Xan's hand although he hadn't landed a blow. I understood why when Crow's blade gleamed red in the moonlight. Logan dropped my hand and hurried away.

"Magi suck." Crow chuckled. "Can't even heal."

With Logan away, I put up my dukes and conjured. Or at least, tried to. My hands flushed briefly with heat that fizzled out almost immediately.

Even if none of my magic worked, my extra sense did. Crow's weapon was enhanced somehow.

"Magic knife!"

"He's scared of a fair fight." Xan chuckled. "Coward."

"You're dead!" Crow snarled. He slashed again, this time at his opponent's face.

Xan ducked and attempted a leg sweep, but Crow hopped aside. Toward me.

I made my move. Nothing fancy, just a slap at his wrist. It worked. I jumped back as the knife flew from his hand and skidded along the deck, past Arick, and out of range.

Xan popped up with a left hook that finally connected and knocked Crow's jaw askance with a *crack*. The green glow on impact meant he'd conjured poison. Unfortunately, even shifters of the bird variety had an advantage magi didn't.

Crow shook his head, and the side of his face straightened out again. He'd already healed the bone, and my extra sense told me his body had already handled the toxin.

I conjured fire and took a step closer, but with Cadence and Xan so close I feared hitting them. Crow knew enough about fighting to sense that, too.

With one hand, he grabbed Xan by the throat and squeezed. Not with the flat of his palm, either, but digging in with his fingers. Like he intended to tear his throat out. Asceco came to her magus's rescue, striking from her hiding place in his shirt. Crow only laughed.

"Basilisk venom? Against a shifter? Don't make me laugh."

I banished the fire and prepared to conjure solar, hoping to blind Crow long enough for Xan to break free.

Three things happened at the same time.

Logan returned, shoes squeaking on the deck as he pointed at the fighting pair.

Bar appeared from under cover of a glamour, fist smashing Crow's wrist like a sledgehammer, releasing Xan.

Cadence lost her balance and grabbed at her ex-boyfriend's trench coat. She missed and went over the side.

An instant later, Dylan skidded to a hard stop against the railing, frantically conjuring air in a last-ditch attempt to stop the banished mermaid from hitting the forbidden deep water.

He was too late.

The rest of us rushed to the side and gazed down into the water, the shock of what had just happened ending the fight. Xan and Bar couldn't possibly have known how dire this situation was for Cadence. Bar frantically searched for a float or a life vest.

Boat security arrived. Xan pointed out the knife, the wound on his hand, and Arick. The burly guard slapped cuffs on Crow. The kind that stopped shifters from changing form.

Logan, Dylan, and I knew there were worse consequences than cold water, concussions, and handcuffs. I stood, clutching my stomach because I sensed some vast and powerful force coming.

Crow did too. His reaction was the opposite of mine.

I knew from both the sickeningly excited hum of his mind and the rapt expression of fascination on his face.

Down in the water, Cadence shook her head. It was the last thing I saw her do before the depths rose beneath her. An enormous limb, spotted and covered with tentacles, obscured her face as it lifted her over the water. All we could see were the red-gold tips of her tail fins.

The rest of the creature rose, its massive bulk still mostly underwater but nearly the size of the ship we stood on. Logan and I identified it at the same time.

"Kraken," we both whispered.

Classmates, teachers, and trustees filed in behind us, all connected by a growing sense of alarm. Understandable, since the boat rocked, moved by the displaced water. Almost everyone stepped back from the railing.

It towered above us at first, then brought its head down. Atop it sat a figure, nearly as burly as Bar, wearing a crown of coral. His beard was turquoise with white streaks, and he had green scales on his tail.

"Since she entered the water on her own, the DelMar daughter will pay for her parents' crime of abducting and slaying my companion's child." He stroked the kraken's glistening skin. "You'll lift anchor and leave her with me."

"It wasn't her fault!" My hands balled into fists. "She fell in by accident."

"Was she pushed?" the merman inquired.

"She was threatened." I pointed at Crow. "He attacked her. But no, she wasn't pushed when she fell."

"My decision stands."

"She's my student." Stephanie Hawkins stepped forward. "I'm responsible for her safety. Take me instead."

"That doesn't satisfy our grievance. A dhampyr is no substitute for what the DelMars took from us. You have no connection to the incident."

"I do." Logan stood in front of us all. "The theft of that egg had everything to do with me."

"Shut your mouth!" Leo Pierce strode toward his son. "Stop talking now."

"No, Dad." Logan trembled like a leaf but held his head high. "I'll own my mistakes. Sir, I've got something to say."

"Speak your piece, magus." The merman raised one hand. Leo had no choice but to back off.

"Not to you." Logan pointed at the kraken. "To her."

I'd never heard sounds like the ones out of Logan's mouth at that moment. Maybe nobody who lived on land had ever made them. I don't think anyone other than me understood the sentiment.

Logan apologized. By the time he finished, he'd dropped to his knees with his hands raised, palms up. Tears streamed down his face.

Now, nobody could deny his talent for speaking to magical creatures. Not after he'd just had an entire conversation with something as mysterious and rare as a kraken.

"From the bottom of my heart, sir, I apologize."

"For?" The merman blinked.

"Not being good enough to bond with the hatchling. I think I could have saved her if I'd managed. So it's my fault. Let Cadence go and punish me instead."

"Young magus, please rise."

Logan did while wiping his nose on his sleeve.

"The lore you land-dwellers have on us is scarce by design, but you must know this. Kraken can only bond with merfolk. Your gifts are undeniably strong, but no magus could have managed that. Cadence DelMar is not responsible. So, we release her from punishment."

The kraken's tentacle unfurled and set Cadence on the deck.

Mermaids sometimes lost their lower garments when shifting unexpectedly. Cadence's legs remained a tail for a moment, which gave me time to remove my jacket and wrap it around her waist. Izzy did the same so she was completely covered. She leaned between us, sobbing.

"A price must be paid." Everything went silent. I looked up. "A child for a child is my thinking. That is the way of the sea."

Leo nodded, one corner of his mouth upturned.

"What?" Logan stared up at his father, eyes wide open. "Dad. No."

"You brought this on yourself," he scoffed. "I warned you."

The tentacle reached for Logan. Doris yowled and bounded in front of Leo where she hissed and spit, tail lashing. Brand the phoenix dove at the mercat, talons out and wings blazing.

"I wish for Leo to pay this price. And suffer for it."

Andre Gauthier stood in the middle of all the chaos with a brass lamp glowing in his hands. A figure shimmered into existence beside him. I recognized her from Logan's description. The woman from the library.

"I'm sorry." The handsome woman waved her hand as a tear trickled down her face.

"It seems my companion wants a different sort of justice from your family," the merman said.

The kraken's appendage hung in midair, then descended again, this time in front of Leo, where Brand did battle with Doris.

I heard a hiss, a scuffle, and a caw. Leo blocked my view of the kraken's tentacle. Logan cried out as the air around him trembled with pain. A fine mist fell on his face, tears in the rain. The tentacle lifted something off the deck—two bundles, gray and still. Finally, the massive creature and her merman sank beneath the water, slowly enough that the boat barely rocked.

Logan fell to the deck and curled up on his side. Despair came off him in waves. My breath caught in my throat. Elanor approached her father with her hands ablaze.

"What did you do?"

"What any reasonable person would have." He banished her conjure. "They were only animals."

I pulled Logan's head into my lap, where he wept in silence. I'd seen this before a year ago, with Dorian.

Doris was gone. Brand, too. Sacrificed in place of Logan himself. Leo Pierce hadn't flinched through any of it, although Andre's wish stipulated his pain.

He'll hurt. Eventually.

All our research told us that wishes always came home to roost. The voice's truth offered cold comfort.

Somewhere behind me, I heard that low intense voice again, chuckling.

CHAPTER EIGHT

We all sat in the infirmary the next morning with Logan asleep in one bed and Hal getting his infusion in another. Hal's chair stood in a corner, a satchel filled with the books and papers from the other day slung across the back.

"I don't get it." Dylan scratched his head. "Why the conference?"

"Everybody knows now that Gauthier had Grandma's lamp," Hal said. "That must have been his last wish."

"So where is it now?" Faith asked.

"Well, one thing's certain," Xan gazed at his bandaged hand. "The wrong people don't have it."

"How do you figure?" Grace asked.

"I know them too well." He tapped his temple. "Things wouldn't be this peaceful if they had their way. They'll find it eventually. Then, we're screwed."

"I know what we all need." Hal smiled. "Coffee and pastry."

"What?" I blinked.

"Normally, I never say no to food." Dylan shook his head. "This is a crisis. Leaving now is madness."

"Risky maybe, but not madness," Hal said. "Trust me on this. We need Witches Brew breakfast. For morale. Nurse Smith and Ian are both here. Logan will be okay."

"I don't want to leave him." I patted Logan's hand. "But Xan's right. So is Hal. We need some breakfast, fresh air, and space to breathe."

When Ian came in to disconnect Hal's infusion, I took Logan's hand and kissed his forehead.

"I'll be back in a bit, dear."

He didn't make a sound or open his eyes, but his hand squeezed mine before we let go. The trauma of losing a familiar affected each magus differently. Logan's talent probably made it harder for him.

Hal kept moving his chair right past Witches Brew and crossed Front Street without stopping, then crossed Derby, which resulted in a lot of head-scratching. Dylan looked longingly over his shoulder at Engine House, which hadn't opened yet.

The entire way, Hal held his phone in his lap, sending texts. He stopped on Washington Street until he read a response, then crossed into The Point.

"They're not going to let me into N—"

"Don't worry, Xan." Hal tucked his phone back in his pocket. "He already said it's okay."

My brother let us into his apartment, finger to his lips. Nobody spoke until we were inside the warded practice room.

"Now that we're in here, they won't know what we say, not even if they've bugged us."

"Are you honestly worried about that?" Grace raised an eyebrow. "Never mind. It's wishes."

"My father would kill to get his hands on that lamp." Faith clenched her fists. "It vanished, so that means it has no master until the next person picks it up."

"Next person who isn't Andre Gauthier or Richard Hopewell, yeah." Hal nodded. "Dad used to joke that the decorations on lamps are actually ancient djinn for no repeat business."

"So, how do we keep it away from him?"

"That lamp's directly connected to my family," Hal said. "It's barely functional, but I'm still a space magus and I'm related by blood."

"Isn't it the same for the headmaster?" Xan asked.

"Nope. He married up." Hal grinned. "Only related to the Haddads by marriage."

"What about your dad?"

"Technically, yes. But he's off-campus today, dealing with the boat charter company. It's pretty safe to assume we lost our deposit."

"You planned this." I nodded. "Since last night when you saw the lamp vanish."

"Exactly." He nodded.

"Don't you need big amplification devices to track something like a lamp though?" Noah asked.

"No, nothing like that." Hal grinned. "Turns out, I've got space affinity. I'm low on power because of my anemia, even right after this morning's infusion. But I learned a trick thanks to Logan, from that green dragon journal he's translated. Just need the wards in here and a little help from you all in the magic department."

Hal pulled an atlas out from under the blanket in his lap and turned to the table of contents. Then, he took a pendulum from his pocket and looped the end of the chain around his middle and ring fingers. He held it above the printed page and stared at it while conjuring.

Sweat beaded on his forehead. Nin sat on his shoulder and pressed her cheek against his. Faith took his free hand, then reached for Grace's with her empty one. I got the idea and laid one of my hands on his shoulder and grabbed Noah's with the other. We formed a circle, gently conjuring and passing the energy of our elements around.

It reminded me of the calming exercise Elanor taught me for Bishop's Row, but somehow, our elements channeled together despite some of them opposing each other.

Faith squeezed Hal's hand. "Go on, ask."

"What page?"

The pendulum swung, defying the laws of physics.

"Ninety." Hal let the bob rest in his lap and flipped through the atlas. "Now, where in Salem?"

The pendulum swung back and forth over Essex Street, eventually coming to rest on the spot by CVS, where the door was today. Faith was prepared. She pulled out a sketch on notebook paper, a map of campus. Hal drew a deep breath and began again.

The pendulum swung past the infirmary and the trustees' quarters, swinging back and forth between the academic wing and student housing. It slowed over the dorms, which Faith hadn't replicated to show every floor. Hal dropped his hand and leaned back in the chair, panting like he'd run wind sprints.

"Do any of the trustees have access there?" Faith asked. "I thought it was off-limits."

"It's lax enough for my mom to knock on my door whenever she's in the bottle," Xan said.

"There are restrictions, though." I chewed my lower lip while thinking. "What was it the headmaster said at the welcome speech? Something about detection wards."

Someone knocked on the door.

"What the hell?" Noah opened it to reveal Elanor.

"Brianna called. It's an emergency. We have to go back to Hawthorn. Now."

"Elanor, we're doing serious sh—"

"Shut up, Noah!" She clutched her phone to her chest. "It's Logan. My dad put him in a car outside the Essex Street Garage. He was unconscious."

"Where?" I shouldered past my brother.

"Nobody knows." She trembled. "And he was bleeding."

Most of us hurried back to campus, where I acted as Elanor's escort. Dylan asked Brianna to stay on Essex Street, so we'd have someone watching the door to message Faith and Hal, who'd stayed behind with Noah at the apartment. He was too bushed to make the trip back without rest, even in the chair. Noah had no choice but to hide from the sun.

We needed information so we split up, intending to ask everyone around what they'd seen or heard. Dylan went to the infirmary, Xan to the café, Dorian the cafeteria, and Grace the dorms. I escorted Elanor to the office, where she pounded on the headmaster's door. He opened it and stared at us with a face like stone.

"Where's my brother?"

"I suggest you ask a relative, Miss Pierce." He shook his head. "I'm unable to discuss medical matters about any Hawthorn students. Privacy, you know."

"We're estranged."

"All the more reason I can't tell you. You're a grown woman, Miss Pierce. Act like it, and handle your family business."

"Sir," I stepped in. "Logan's estranged from them. He's an adult too. So, please. We only want to know where he is, to make sure he's safe."

"He's in the care of medical professionals."

"That's not good enough." The air around Elanor heated up. "I happen to know he left in a car, not an ambulance."

"I'm sorry I can't do more, Miss Pierce. Please. Find *a relative*. It's the only way." He closed the door.

She stalked out of the hall and through the lobby, making a beeline for the exit. I jogged to get in front of her, then turned around and walked backward.

"Stop, Elanor. Think."

"About what?"

"Why was he so insistent about a relative?" I pushed the vestibule door open with my hands behind my back. "I mean, he could have said your father if that's who he meant."

"Mom's in Vegas. The only other relative I have around here is locked up." She kept walking toward the exterior door.

"Wait." I stopped so abruptly she almost ran into me. "Do you mean your aunt? Petra?"

"How did you know about her?" She blinked. "Even Logan doesn't—"

I pushed the door open and stood with her in front of CVS,

explaining about the yearbook. Including how Gamila gave it to Logan in the library.

"Don't say another word, ladies." Andre Gauthier emerged from the school door. "Not with Lavinia about to walk out for brunch. Follow me, and we can help each other."

He led us down the street to the parking garage and into the long-term section. We turned a corner to a row where only one vehicle stood. He drove an old-fashioned hearse of course, from the 1970s and in mint condition. As we approached, two people stepped out from behind the car. Bubbe and Izzy.

"Mildred Morgenstern?" Mr. Gauthier blinked.

"You don't bring Aliyah anywhere without me, Andre."

"It's not your business."

"My grandkid, my business." She crossed her arms over her chest. "I've got a Mendez soothsayer contradicting you."

"Hi." Izzy let out a nervous giggle. "My *abuela* says you ignored her warnings back in the day and that I shouldn't help you. When I said it's for Bubbe, she gave her blessing. Anyway, everything goes up in smoke if you go in a trio. You need four or more."

"Success means two more passengers later." Mr. Gauthier frowned. "It's not legal to drive with anyone in the back who isn't dead. I won't have room if I bring you all."

"Then Bubbe stays in Salem." Izzy's hands trembled.

"No, you do." Bubbe raised an eyebrow. "We discussed this already, Isabella."

"But the cards said—"

"You stay. I go."

"If you're sure."

"I am."

"Fine." Izzy swallowed. "See you, then. When I see you."

This does not bode well.

There wasn't any time to press Izzy for more information or my grandmother for that matter. Bubbe got in the passenger side. I got in the back with Elanor. The car had bench seats, so there'd be space for two more if we all squeezed. I wondered at first why one seat wasn't enough. Until Mr. Gauthier pointed the car toward Danvers and Elanor's response brought the headmaster's words into precise focus for both of us.

"The Sanitarium?" She gasped. "Aunt Petra!"

"Yes. Where the Pierces have always put their rebels. Now hold on." Mr. Gauthier stepped on the gas. "This is a race."

"I don't get it." But I did. He was as cautious as Hal and didn't want his enemies to know where he was going. I should have been more careful. There was nothing I could do now besides keep quiet about the lamp.

And hope any damage my loose lips had done stayed at a minimum.

The Sanitarium in Danvers was a sprawling brick building set in the middle of a bucolic green lawn. The granite steps glittered in the late morning sun, dazzling my eyes as we went up them and through sliding glass doors. The floor and walls were wide planks, bleached like driftwood. The only decor in the immediate area were long stalks of something like bamboo in alabaster planters, which both Andre and Bubbe side-eyed immediately.

I'm not sure what I'd expected the inside to look like, but the reality was nothing like what they show in the movies. No glass laced with metal, no bars, no mundane barriers of any kind that the eye could see, besides a half-wall that reminded me of the Dutch doors in Bubbe's office.

There were no apparent gates, catches, or latches in that low wall, which was painted to resemble fieldstone. I saw no desk or any attendants. People of all shapes, sizes, and ages moved on the other side, dressed in soft pastel pants and tops, reminding me of Monet's *Garden*.

They went about the business of living gently, oblivious to our presence by the entrance. When I approached the wall and tried leaning over it to catch the nearest person's attention, a ward stopped me. The patient in question, a lanky bald man older than Bubbe, moved along as though I were invisible.

I peered at them and noticed something else that didn't track with my clearly incorrect assumptions about inpatient mental health care. Nobody looked unkempt or otherwise in distress. Some sat, others paced, and a few engaged in repetitive behaviors with hands or feet. Most seemed alert and engaged in some activity or other. Reading, or artwork, or board games, or cards. One snored faintly in a reclining chair with a cozy blanket draped over her legs. Another dozed over a magazine at a small table. As I watched, the wood beneath him shifted to match the angle of the other sleeper's seat. A blanket appeared as if by magic and tucked itself under his arms as the magazine settled in his lap, page unturned.

If the people made me think of Monet, the murals put me in mind of Van Gogh. The artwork stretched from top to bottom, with magical creatures as the most frequent subjects. There was one that featured a rainbow-hued flight of dragonets, the largest one eerily similar to Ember.

I tried picking out the dominant magical energy in the room, but so many types mingled that it was next to impossible.

"Yeah, she's here all right." Mr. Gauthier chuckled at the artwork. "I should have known. Wouldn't have needed Gamila at all if it weren't for Dishonest Abe and his blasted mind magic. Which, of course, is part and parcel of how she wound up in this place."

"I thought we were here for my kin." Elanor glared.

"Oh, we are." He nodded.

"So, exactly how are you helping?" I raised an eyebrow.

"As a chauffeur, of course." He grinned like the Cheshire Cat. "Besides, young Mr. Pierce is in here. And he owes me a favor."

"What's this really about, Andre?" Bubbe had her arms crossed over her chest.

"Why, Petra of course, Mildred."

"I should have known." Bubbe seemed to deflate. "Well, go on then. Rescue her if you've finally got the means."

"You know as well as I do that's not how the Sanitarium works. First, we've got to get in."

"That takes blood." Bubbe nodded.

I rummaged in my bag for something sharp.

"No, Aliyah." Elanor put her hand on my arm. "Watch this."

She walked over to the wall and placed her hand on the top, where one of the painted stones appeared to have a sharp edge. She wrinkled her nose, and when she took her hand away, I saw a tiny drop of blood.

"Pierce?" A voice called, but nobody appeared. "One of you passed this way a short time ago."

"I'm here for my brother Logan," Elanor said. "My Aunt Petra, too."

"I'm afraid Mr. Logan's still in eval for the next while. You're welcome to visit with Miss Petra while you wait."

"Thanks." She beckoned. "Come on."

"I'm sorry, but only family is permitted entry." The voice carried a hint of sadness.

"I was Logan's legal guardian for a year." Bubbe said. "That must count for something."

"I am Miss Petra's fiancé," Andre added.

"Please hold."

A bland tune in major key played softly.

"Miss Elanor Pierce, Mr. Andre Gauthier. Miss Petra is in the lounge."

"What about my brother?"

"Your visit time with your aunt matches the remaining time in his evaluation."

They walked directly toward a stretch of wall between two planters, as though it were a door. They passed through. I tried following, hand outstretched, but my fingers met wood.

"Glamour," Bubbe said.

"How? Nobody's out here."

"Brownies." She jerked her chin at the planters. "This place is fae-run."

"Whoa." I blinked, then thought of Logan. They'd said he was still in eval. I wondered, did that mean Leo was here with him? Were decisions being made, long-term ones, at this very moment?

Yes. You need to act now.

Short of threatening mass murder by lighting up brownies, I couldn't think of a way in.

"Bubbe, what do we do?"

"First, tell me about this deal with Andre."

I did. And what we'd overheard about the conservatorship.

"Then we need to get in there immediately."

"That's what I've been saying. But how?"

"Brownies follow rules, but they use intellect to interpret them. Letting Andre in means there's wiggle room on their interpretation of family." She tapped her temple. "Convince them."

"Oh!"

Don't get me wrong. It wasn't like I forgot about having mind magic. I had the worst teacher, so I wasn't sure when to try using it. Mr. Fairbanks had turned my training to his advantage. Professor Hawkins wasn't sure how it worked or what to do with it, but my education wasn't limited to either of them, thank goodness.

I thought back to Professor Luciano. He always told us to trust the process of our magic.

When in doubt, call on it and see what happens.

With all the vulnerable patients around, even behind wards, that was a risk I almost didn't take. However, professors weren't my only teachers. I was captain of the Bishop's Row team, bound for college on a scholarship because of my skill. Mind magic was like any other energy. Conjurable.

I held my hands up and together, focused on bringing my third magic forward.

I failed.

Fire bloomed between my palms instead. I banished it and tried again. Light took its place, and I shook my head. The third time, I felt with my fingers that it worked although I couldn't see any hint of an orb. Mind energy was more difficult to see than Faith's undeath.

"What do I do with it?"

Glancing from the space between my hands to the stretch of wall between the planters, I stood stumped.

Throwing an orb, even one made from mind magic, was a direct attack on the caretakers here. From what I'd observed, the brownie staff operated with care and kindness. It wasn't their fault that some people were here under coercion from malicious family members. They didn't deserve aggression from me and acting out like this might only support Leo Pierce's arguments that his son wasn't safer with his chosen family.

I needed to focus the energy, not aim and fire it. So I had no choice but to banish the orb.

In your bag.

The ear cuffs.

I fished them out and put them on, wincing at the pinching they made in my rush. A chuckle at the irony of this situation bubbled up from my throat. Was I using my shackles to help set someone else free? Yes. Yes, I was.

Approaching one of the planters put me beside the wall, which I realized at once was made up of brownies. I beckoned to Bubbe, who joined me. We held hands. Then, I rested my palm on the surface in front of me, remembering all the years I'd spent getting to know Logan.

Bubbe came along memory lane with me, which had more than one unintended effect. She saw me at my worst in a few of them. Then she added in some of hers. Together, we made a kaleidoscope of experience, projected through the connection the ear cuffs made between the brownies and my magic.

Logan in the Hawthorn lobby, taking my breath away the first time I saw him. How he set fear of his family aside and saved Doris. The calm comfort he offered through our first year when I feared discovery as an extramagus. His face under the sodium lamp that night in Salem, trusting me when he had nowhere else to go. Bubbe signing below his signature on a paper at Salem District Court, and the handshake that became a hug.

The kindness he offered to every guest in second year. His brilliance in the classroom and in Lab. How he never left my side, even through the horror of Temperance and Luciano's death. Kindness and comfort, given to strangers at Bubbe's practice. Interceding to save Cadence, which was how he ended up here in the first place.

"Curious. That's not what his father said."

I opened my eyes with some small amount of difficulty. My lashes were laden with tears, but I saw clearly enough through them to realize I wasn't in the lobby of Danvers Sanitarium anymore.

"You did it, Aliyah." Bubbe gestured at a long table, where Logan sat beside Leo at a bench staring at a pen, a folder open in front of him.

"We." I shook my head. "Including him. All of that, what I showed them, came from his choices."

Logan didn't look up, like the fellow I'd tried interacting with when I'd first arrived there. As though he couldn't hear or see us.

"I thought we'd get to, you know, visit with him," I said to nobody in particular.

"As recent family, this is what we can do," the voice said.

"Perhaps it'd make a difference if he could see us here." Bubbe raised an eyebrow.

"Done."

The light changed, warmed somehow. Leo noticed us. Logan still didn't look up.

"Don't you see now? All those rules, everything I did. It's because I knew you couldn't manage on your own."

"I'm still top of the class, Dad." He turned his head to look at his father. "I did that all by myself."

"Academics are only more rules. When something goes wrong, who's going to bail you out?"

"Aliyah always rescues me." He swallowed, tears rolling down his cheek. "She loves me, Dad. More than you do, I think."

"Come home, and if you do everything as I say, you'll always have a roof over your head." He didn't even glance in our direction but picked the pen up and placed it in Logan's hand. "Sign it. That girl's not here for you now, when it counts."

The voice sounded in sing-song. "Falsehood detected."

"I meant to say, where is she now?"

Logan turned his head. Leo held up his hand as if he'd slap him. Instead, he cupped it, trying to stop him from seeing us. With his other hand, Leo held his son's wrist, guiding it toward the paper.

"Just sign it."

I held my hands out, pressed them against the same sort of invisible barrier that held me back.

"Logan!" I screamed his name, making fists and pounding on the wards. Sparks flew with each beat. "Don't sign!"

Finally, he saw me and his face lit up, as though he could conjure solar magic behind his eyes. He dropped the pen.

"No, Dad." He grinned and conjured water that flowed over the contract, washing away ink and soaking through the paper. "Never."

"Evaluation complete. Outpatient therapy recommended."

He rushed to us and embraced Bubbe briefly first, then me. He stood between us, one arm around my waist. Leo stood and glowered.

"I'm out too, Leo." Petra strode through another ward on the other side of the room, Andre and Elanor behind her.

"What? How?" Mr. Pierce's face went an alarming shade of red.

"It's right here in your contract." Andre chuckled and produced an almost identical paper, this one with yellowed edges. "I did my research. Release form's only valid if a blood relative signs it."

"Elanor?" He drew the name out, raising his voice as he spoke, making the end sound like a roar.

"Yeah. Aunt Petra's a free woman. You're a monster."

"You want a monster?" His hands blazed. "I'll show you a monster."

Leo Pierce conjured an inferno. This time, it was more than double the size of the one I'd banished years ago in Lab, and Ember was back at Hawthorn, on her nest.

I immediately started banishing. So did Elanor, and Fifi who rose from her shoulder. It felt like standing in front of Mr. Ambersmith's blast furnace. I even smelled hair burning. Logan and Petra conjured water, trying to extinguish what we couldn't banish. Bubbe put her hand on my shoulder, lending me strength. Andre did the same for Elanor. It wouldn't be enough.

Mr. Pierce was almost godlike in his magic, beyond imagining. Logan told me once that his entrance music on stage was *Walking on the Sun*. I'd thought it bluster, but I'd been wrong. His fire burned so hot it was blue, a color I'd never seen from my hands or anyone else's.

The ear cuffs gave me a single advantage. Banishing an element someone else conjured was almost like touching them. So I knew his intentions.

Leo Pierce would burn the entire sanitarium down before seeing his sister and son walk out of it under their power. He almost got his way.

Blue drowned out red, but white was brighter.

Bubbe pointed at Leo and flashed light in his eyes. His flames faltered and guttered. A vine-like length of charred wood rose from the table, splintered and dripping a clear sap. It reared back like a striking serpent and punctured his arm. When he lifted his hands to cast again, it was like on the boat when Crow had that knife. His hands remained empty, his magic subdued.

"Confinement in the aggression ward, stat." The voice stated, much more calmly than expected in a recently burning place made of and run by creatures of wood.

"Oranges. Barcode. Theramin," Bubbe said. Her knees buckled. A bench moved under her as she collapsed, her right arm curling against her chest.

"Calling Emergency Extrahuman Services, Law Enforcement."

In moments, we found ourselves out on the steps, where sirens sounded nearby. People piled out of the ambulance, surrounding Bubbe and hustling her onto a gurney. I tried getting in, but they stopped me. Behind us, police cars pulled up in front of the sanitarium. Elanor ushered us toward the backseat of the restored hearse, where we sat and waited as Andre chased the ambulance.

CHAPTER NINE

Instead of shaking, crying, or even screaming, I reacted with numbness. Was this how an ice magus felt? I wondered as I woke my phone and called my parents. Logan put his arms around me, weeping as I told Mom where we'd been, what had happened, and where we were going.

Salem Hospital's emergency room saw Bubbe immediately, while the rest of us waited. Mom and Dad walked through the door. Noah arrived later, through the stairwell to the basement. A nurse came and brought my father through a set of double doors. My phone beeped with a message from Izzy.

I'm sorry, she sent. And immediately after, the three of swords reversed.

I couldn't text back. She must have done a reading and seen that card, one of the worst in the deck. But the message explained a lot about her argument with Bubbe in the parking garage. I couldn't blame Izzy for what happened. Nobody stopped Mildred Morgenstern when she had her mind set on something. Not even an inauspicious reading from the most talented precognitive family in Salem.

Dad emerged from the double doors. He gathered Mom, me, Noah, and Logan, then took us aside.

"I'm sorry." Logan stared at the floor.

"Nobody here blames you." Dad patted his shoulder. "Bubbe's had a stroke, but they got her here in time. Doc says she's six points on THRIVE."

"Um, can you explain that, Dad?" Noah blinked back tears. "Not a medical person here."

"It means she'll have a good outcome after recovery and therapy, but it'll take time and a lot of work. Her life might be a little different even after that." He reached out and tried to put his arms around us all. We crowded in, faces all covered with tears. Logan stood still between my mom and me, shaking.

"Hey." I rubbed his back. "Hey. What's wrong?"

"She wouldn't be in there if it wasn't for—"

"Your father." Mom looked up and wiped her eyes. "If he'd left you in the infirmary as he was supposed to, everything would have been fine. You can't blame yourself. Bubbe made sure I didn't when I was your age. Her advice is timeless. Let's honor it. Now, tell us what happened."

Logan's mouth dropped open. He looked from her to me, then at Dad and Noah. Everybody nodded.

"Nurse Smith gave me Valium last night. It wore off in his car, in the sanitarium parking lot. I was bleeding." He held up one bandage-covered forearm. "The brownies asked me a lot of questions about Doris, how I felt, asking if I still wanted to hurt myself. Dad kept insisting I wasn't safe at Hawthorn. He said he saw me try to cut my wrists in the infirmary. I almost believed him, too. Then he lied about you. Said you wouldn't come because you don't care about me. I knew that was wrong. Well, you heard all that. You were there."

"We called Nurse Smith," Dad said. "He cared for Dorian just fine last year, and you were getting the same treatment. So we knew he had everything under control."

"Right." Elanor cleared her throat. "I called the infirmary, too. You were on Ms. Khan's schedule and everything. Then Dad happened because he's a malicious son of a bitch."

"Language." Mom raised an eyebrow. "But yes. He hasn't stopped trying to sabotage Logan over the last two years. You just didn't see the paperwork." She shook her head, then gazed at Logan. "Did you sign anything while at Danvers Sanitarium?"

"No, Mrs. Morgenstern." He shook his head. "He had papers and kept pushing a pen at me. Bubbe and Aliyah got there before I did."

"Well, that's a blessing." She sighed. "Where are the documents now?"

"Burned up when he went nuclear," Elanor said.

"What?" Mom's eyes widened.

"Ask Aunt Petra."

We turned toward the seat where she sat holding hands with Andre. She resembled Logan, with the same hair and the eyes that escaped meeting gazes. While Logan reminded me of the ocean, Petra put me in mind of the time we vacationed at Niagara-on-the-Lake. We sat as each of us explained our part in the whole incident. When we finished, everyone took a few moments to process it all.

"Excuse me." Dad rose. "I'm telling all of this to Bubbe's doctors. Any information about how it happened can only help them."

Andre followed, but only to get a cup of water from the cooler in the waiting area. He popped what looked like a Tylenol capsule in his mouth and washed it down before pacing back over. He rubbed the bridge of his nose.

"So, my dad did the same thing to you?" Logan asked.

"Not him." Petra shook her head. "Our father. But that's probably where he got the idea for a conservatorship."

"Why?"

"You hear them too, right?" She grinned. "The animals. All of them. I used to do a translation act. One night, I couldn't stand it. I told them how the creatures in the menagerie really felt and spoke their misery. They brought me to Danvers and made me sign."

"So how come you weren't at their compound in Vegas?"

"I refused to leave the Sanitarium. As you saw, it's a kind sort of place. I might have been behind walls, but I was free of them." She glanced up at Andre. "I wasn't as forgotten as I'd feared."

"Please excuse my unacceptable tardiness." He bowed and held out his hand. She took it.

"We'll see." She squeezed his hand. "But I think you're in the clear."

The hospital admitted Bubbe and gave us information about visiting hours. Nurse Smith arrived to bring Logan directly back to the infirmary. Noah and Elanor headed back to their apartment through the tunnel. Mom and Dad drove me back to campus.

As we walked out of Salem Hospital, my phone *beeped* with a message from Grace. Only while checking it did I realize that the cafeteria at school hadn't finished serving lunch yet. Time moved strangely in a crisis.

Police at school. Make statement, meet me in our room.

Logan headed downstairs to the infirmary. I sat with the representative from Salem PD in the lounge corner that had been cordoned off with a fancy velvet rope.

"This is the second time in as many days that you're giving a statement, Morgenstern." Detective Ambersmith raised an eyebrow. "Should I be concerned for your safety?"

"No, ma'am." I shook my head. "I'm more worried about my friends. It's Mr. Fairbanks. He's dangerous."

"With good reason, I should say." She glanced down at the statement she'd copied. "I never liked the idea of those trustees being here. If it had all gone down on campus, I'd call the school board and ask for a shutdown and full inquiry."

"Well, it didn't, but we have exams starting Monday and—"

"Aliyah." She blinked. "You always took school seriously. I remember you trying to do Noah's homework back when I used to be your babysitter, but this is ridiculous. I'm talking about life and death here, and you're thinking of grades."

"No, I'm not. There's still a—"

"It's because you're an extramagus." She sighed and nodded. "You think you're tough enough. I get it. So, help me protect your friends. What's the risk at Hawthorn? For real."

"Like I said. Lavinia Onassis gave Crow that knife. Leo Pierce was a time bomb. The knife's gone, and Leo went off at the Sanitarium. Hawthorn Academy runs on space magic, which should have made the headmaster aware. But he wasn't. So Abe Fairbanks must be helping them hide everything with mind magic."

"Leo's staying where he is pending arraignment. You don't have to worry about him at school. Mr. Merlini's waiting on a lawyer, which is his right, so accusations against Mrs. Onassis are hearsay until we know more. Is there anyone else on campus who's a threat?"

"I told you already." I blinked. I'd said the man's name twice.

"No. You didn't."

"I'm trying to tell you. They have a ringleader."

"Go on."

"Mr. Fairbanks. He's still dangerous."

She moved her pen over the statement form, but it didn't make contact. I stared, unable to believe what I was seeing. How could a seasoned detective be unaware of not taking notes? I glanced up and looked toward the lobby entrance, where Andre Gauthier had returned. His eyes fixed on a point to my left. He tensed for a moment, then relaxed and walked in the opposite direction, toward the dorms. Detective Ambersmith cleared her throat.

"Don't you have any other concerns?" She shook her head at the paper again. "Because from what you've said already, there's nothing I can do to increase safety measures."

"Detective, I don't know how to make it any clearer. Abraham Fairbanks is behind—"

There he was, standing by the cream and sugar table and grinning at me. He tapped his temple. I glanced out at the empty lobby, the unattended counter, the unoccupied seats nearby. Then, I burst into tears. Detective Ambersmith set her clipboard aside and patted my shoulder.

"I know, I know." She handed me a tissue. "You're stressed and frightened. It's okay if you can't talk about it right now. I'll be back to talk with Logan on Tuesday after dinner. So, come and meet me then once you've had a rest. Maybe it'll be easier having your boyfriend there."

"Can't I come to the station?" I blew my nose.

"Well, I'm glad you asked that." She sighed and handed me another tissue. "It's not possible. I can't act if we discuss things off-campus. Jurisdiction is weird when it comes to between worlds spaces. The entire investigation has to happen here like it did last year."

"I understand." I wiped my eyes. I did. All too well.

Abe Fairbanks had all his interests cornered, trapped in the pocket dimension that was Hawthorn Academy. He had the means, the power, and the advantage to get everything he wanted without interference.

The lamp that was Hal's last shot at saving his life was the first item on that list.

Upstairs, I filled my friends in on what happened at Danvers Sanitarium and everything that followed, up to the futile police statement. After expressions of relief that Logan was free, Bubbe on the mend, and Leo off the board, we danced along the edge of safe conversation and saying too much.

"With Leo out of the picture, the situation from this morning is even worse."

"How can we properly look if we can't even talk?" Dylan groaned his frustration and flopped back on my bed.

"We'll have to cope with redundancy." Hal sighed. "Running over the same old ground."

"Worst efficiency ever," Faith grumbled. "Zero stars."

"Hmm." Grace peered at me, then pointed at my ear. "Can I see one of those?"

"Uh, okay?" I removed the ear cuffs and handed them over. It wasn't physically possible to forget I was wearing them, but I'd certainly forgotten the fact I could take them off in all the chaos.

Grace took her time while turning the jewelry over in her hands. She rummaged in her desk drawer and brought out a monocle, which she held up to her eye as she continued the examination.

"What are you thinking?" Hal asked.

"See for yourself, magiscience whiz." She handed both items to him.

"This is awesome." After a moment, Hal nodded. "Put them back on, Aliyah."

"Okay?" I took it from him and did.

"Now we huddle up," Grace said.

Once we met in the middle of the room, she put her arms over Dylan's and Faith's shoulders. We all followed suit. A moment later, it all came clear to me.

They'd given me the cuffs to restrict mind magic. I'd learned early on that they enhanced it with contact when I touched Logan while wearing them, but I'd assumed it was partly a quirk of how close we were.

It took a dire emergency for me to deliberately try using them to commune with a stranger, the brownie in Danvers Sanitarium. Grace seized on that immediately and made her theory, that the cuffs also blocked incoming mind magic. I felt her glee when I montaged bits of all the sessions with Mr. Fairbanks, when I'd put the cuffs in their box on the desk. Then, I saw what she did—all our faces.

"It's like Aliyah-Grace-o-vision." Dylan chuckled. "Huh."

"Shh," Hal said. Then I got a cartoonish image of a mustachioed Abe Fairbanks with his forehead on the outside of a door, zig-zags of mean thoughts spiking the wood.

We all laughed.

We didn't have an actual conversation after that, more like a series of brain art. Hal's remained like sketches, while Dylan's resembled music videos complete with a soundtrack. Faith's were verbal, words forming in front of a cursor on a screen. Our thoughts moved faster than speech.

In moments, we had a plan set up to search all eight floors in the dorm for the lamp, even the unused ones. We needed more help but could discuss that without the ear cuff huddle. Everybody knew I was starting to reach my limit.

"Dylan, go get Lee and Dorian. Might as well include Xan if you can find him. Just show them the picture of you know what from our lab notes."

"What about Logan?" I asked. "Should we wait for him to get out of the infirmary?"

"Go to him after we're done here," Hal said. "We can handle this without him if he needs rest."

"We're all sleeping like logs tonight." Dylan chuckled.

"Maybe that's a good thing, with exams and all." Faith shrugged. "Anyway, let's get started."

We managed to search the entire dorm although it took the whole afternoon and part of the evening, up until dinner. None of us found Gamila's lamp. Somebody must have gotten there first. The best-case scenario was one of the first years. The worst, we didn't want to consider.

Dinner was almost over by the time I left Logan in the infirmary. He'd stay overnight, and Ian had already ordered his food from Penelope. I needed to do that for myself so I headed for the cafeteria.

One glance up at the arch in the lobby told me that Ember still sat on her nest. Gale stood watch as she slept there. As I watched, Julia soared up with a bundle of food in her talons. She dropped it off, and Gale immediately opened it, crooning to wake Ember. They shared their meal, an assortment of fish heads from the kitchen.

"Fishhead roulette's not for me." Dorian nudged me with his elbow. "Let's go get the beverage variety. The last thing I want to see is you passing out."

"I miss her."

"I get it." He sighed. "Eventually, old Julia here will feather a nest."

"It's okay to miss her too. Mercy, I mean." We got in line for food.

"I do every day. Like Julia here misses Filberto. And like Logan misses Doris."

"Bubbe won't be able to help him as she did for you."

"I, uh," he tapped his temple. "Heard how she's in the hospital. I'm paying her kindness forward. As soon as Nurse Smith lets him have another visitor."

"Thanks, Dorian."

We ordered our food, pizza slices. After that, we moved to the beverage section where Dorian looked around before speaking again.

"Did Xan really come out of nowhere and fight Crow? Without magic?"

"He didn't say anything?" I watched him get beverage roulette as he spoke.

"No. Not a word, although I asked about that cut on his hand. I went with Lee to the Witch's Brew this morning. He and Izzy told me. So, was it true?"

"Yeah, he did." I gestured at a table in the corner. "Let's sit and talk."

Over lunch, I told him everything. The magic-canceling dagger, Xan's trash talk, how I'd have ended up unconscious on the deck without my magic, like Arick. Dorian leaned across the table. I met him halfway, and he whispered in my ear.

"Okay, so I might be a total idiot. I'm in love." He sat back down, his face the utter picture of serious for once.

"I kinda figured that."

"Was I that obvious?"

"Not really. But everyone talks to me about this kind of thing lately for some reason, so I've been looking for it more."

"It doesn't bother you?"

"No. Should it?"

"When I got here, you two were enemies. I watched you help him despite that. So I figured, if anyone knew whether making big declarations to Xan Onassis is a good idea, it'd be you." He swallowed. "I'm not a total coward anymore, but old habits die hard. I trust your judgment. So, should I tell him?"

"Absolutely."

He nodded, then got up to drop off his tray. I followed him, expecting we'd say see you later, and I'd go upstairs for a nap. Dorian wasn't running on the same track as me. He made a beeline for the café, where Xan was behind the counter on shift. And he did it, right then and there.

Xan blushed but nodded and said something back. I didn't need to hear what, because that connection I'd sensed between the two of them since the masquerade ball flourished like mulberries in July. Kayleigh the manager shooed Xan out from behind the counter and grinned as the pair embraced.

I stood under Ember's arch, smiling until my cheeks hurt. Then I got back on the stairs I showered and went to bed, hoping the morning would bring even more promise.

CHAPTER TEN

Monday birthed exam week, and nothing at all was normal about it.

Someone knocked on my door at four-thirty in the morning. I opened it in rumpled pajamas and bed head, worrying over a medical emergency for either Logan or Hal. Or Ember's eggs hatching. It wasn't any of those things.

"Hi, Aliyah."

Noah stood outside my door. I'd forgotten he was scheduled to move in until after graduation.

"Oh, hi." I shoved my feet into slippers and stepped out of the room where Grace still slept.

"I've got stuff downstairs. Can you help?"

"Um, okay." I rubbed my eyes as I followed him. Then rubbed them again at the stack of suitcases. "It's four days, Noah."

"I'm the first vampire to graduate from here. Making the best impression is an enormous burden."

"So is impressing Dylan," I mumbled.

"Gesundheit." He gave me a fish-eye. "That was a sneeze, right?"

"Anything you say." I yawned and hoisted bags up to my shoulders and snagged a third with wheels, dragging it behind me. "What floor?"

"Down to goblin town." He chuckled. "Infirmary, away!"

"When did you become a morning person?" I groaned.

"This is like after dinner for me now." He grinned. "It's going to suck taking exams at the equivalent of three AM, though."

They'd given him Zeke's old quarters, which was good because a regular dorm room might not have accommodated his wardrobe. A refrigerator stocked with bagged blood sat in the corner, beside a sink and a microwave, amenities the rest of us didn't have. It had a restroom *en suite*, too.

"I've got room envy."

"It's only four days." He winked.

"Can I go back to bed?"

"Why not pop in and see Logan first?"

"Are you kidding? He's asleep."

"Am not." Logan stood in the doorway, rubbing one eye with a knuckle. I perked up immediately.

"How are you?"

"Sleepy. And you?"

"Same." I yawned again. "Do you want a hug?"

He nodded, and I went to his side. We stood there for so long I wasn't sure whether it was real or a dream.

Noah cleared his throat, so it was real. We stepped aside and took seats in the infirmary's waiting room as Noah went to fetch whatever else he needed. Then we went straight from hugging to full cuddle mode.

An alarm woke me later in an infirmary bed. I opened my eyes and immediately saw Logan in the next bed over as he rolled toward me. We sat up and stretched.

"Are you cleared for taking exams?"

"Yeah." He glanced at the clock above the door. "You'd better head upstairs and get dressed, though. You have half an hour before breakfast ends."

We hugged again, and I rushed out to the stairs and up them to my room. I hurried through my morning routine in half the usual time. I barely managed to grab toast before the café closed.

As I headed through the doors to the academic wing, it occurred to me that I hadn't studied at all over the weekend. Or for most of the previous week either.

"Who got the bright idea to have exams right after Bishop's Row?"

"I know, right?" Faith leaned against the wall outside our classroom. "I didn't study."

"You're not alone."

Professor Hawkins let us in after that, and we had the next three hours to mark lettered circles and fill blue books silently. Except Hal finished after an hour, with Dylan ten minutes behind him. Dorian sauntered out right before the two-hour mark, and Faith with a half-hour to spare. Logan was halfway to the front of the room when the professor called time. I set my pencil down and stretched before standing, then headed out of the room and down the hall to Creatives, where everyone else was engrossed in finishing their latest projects. Almost. Grace walked in behind me.

"Thank goodness Lab practicals are tomorrow." She grinned. "My brain feels like a fried egg."

"Mine feels like a spilled smoothie."

"Let's go make something, then."

We did, all the way up to the lunch bell, where I spotted a cluster of middle-aged people arriving on campus, dragging wheeled suitcases toward the entrance to the faculty wing. As the last one entered, I saw Andre Gauthier hustle out before the door closed. He glanced at me and nodded as he power-walked directly toward the academic wing.

Not a peep from that man's mind.

The phenomenon was so curious, I turned around and greeted him.

"Hey, Mr. Gauthier." I gave him my most adult-friendly grin. "Do you need help with anything?"

"Er, ah." He slowed his pace, seeming a bit more winded than he should have been. "No, not really. Just late to, hmm, audit a first-year lab."

"Okay, see you later." I stopped following him halfway across the lobby.

Don't buy that story for a minute.

I didn't. So I did my best to focus, trying to break through whatever wall he had up. I couldn't. The barrier, whatever it was, felt springy and flexible, not anything rigid. So, it was shatter-proof.

Fairbanks-proof too, I'd wager.

The answers to how Andre protected his thoughts and what he was doing while shielded would have to wait. My stomach grumbled, so I hurried back to my friends.

"Are parents visiting for graduation already?" I nudged Hal as we entered the cafeteria.

"Not exactly." He shook his head. "Leo's not coming back. So we're missing a trustee. That's the last of the out-of-town alumni arriving to cast votes, but it's a technicality. I already told Logan his mother arrived this morning. She's the only one qualified for the spot."

"What about my mom or dad? Couldn't one of them try for it?"

"Neither of them are the oldest alumnus in your family." He sighed. "If Bubbe weren't still recovering, she'd be eligible. Same with my grandpa, if he weren't headmaster."

"Wow. I had no idea that was part of the requirements. Are you worried?"

"I keep telling myself at least it's not Mrs. Fairbanks."

"Why not Petra? She's older than Mrs. Pierce, I thought."

"No secondary degree." Hal shrugged. "I don't like it, but there's nothing we can do. There's only one good thing about this."

"Which is?"

"The trustees will be occupied through the meeting, vote, and most of the night getting her up to speed. We'll have no trouble from them, at least."

The fact that I didn't have any more sessions scheduled with Mr. Fairbanks was an enormous relief although the idea of Logan's mother as the new trustee still galled me. After dinner, as I watched the crowd of visiting alumni leave, I felt a little better.

Hal turned out to be correct. Mr. Fairbanks gave us no trouble at all. At least, not for the remainder of Monday.

Tuesday was another story entirely.

I woke early the next morning before it would have been light out in Salem. Grace still slept, so I dressed and went to the bathroom to brush my teeth. After that, I headed downstairs and into the twilit lobby, staring at the darkened cafeteria.

"Hey, you." Noah stepped through the doors to the academic wing.

"What are you doing up?"

"Just finished the Lab practical."

"Oh, they didn't let you take it in the library?"

"They would have, but I didn't want to make the professors set the entire thing up in two places so I got it done before sunrise." He cleared his throat although vampires don't have to do that. "I'll get us both in trouble if I say more. But there's a shockingly important item in there."

"Huh?" The only important magical item I could think of on this campus was Gamila's lamp. I banished the thought the moment after it entered my mind. Noah had all but told me someone was listening.

"I can't say more." He tugged his earlobe and glanced at the wall. "Don't want anyone thinking I'm passing you answers. Or anything."

"That's nice of you." I nodded. "Hey, for accommodations, couldn't they have covered the windows and let you take it with the rest of us instead?"

"Andre Gauthier insisted." He shook his head. "He said it might have been embarrassing. I'm required to wear gloves. Something about preventing accidental use of vampire senses to identify things, but it felt like their typical brand of prejudice. Anyway, it's over now. I'm going to bed. It's tiring, keeping two sets of waking hours."

"Won't you have to do that in college?"

"Oxford Occult offers every course of study through their Night School."

"So you accepted?"

"I'm leaning that way. It's hard to say no to a full scholarship at the world's oldest English-speaking magical school." He gave me a half-smile. "Dylan's going. So, there's that."

"What *is* that, exactly?"

"I don't ask you to define things with Logan."

"That's fair." I raised an eyebrow. "I think there's a difference between defying definitions that don't fit and being cautious."

"Which is wise in both our cases."

"You sound like Bubbe. It looks good on you."

"Ditto, kiddo."

The lights came on in the cafeteria. We spoke at the same time, but not entirely over each other.

"Get your rest."

"Get those grades." Noah chuckled. "Love you."

"Love you too."

We went our separate ways for the day.

I had breakfast before everyone else, then got my gym uniform and headed off to run laps because my nerves wouldn't let me sit still. The fine spray of water in the shower washed away sweat but not anxiety. This was an enormously important day academically, but it felt like more than a difficult exam was coming.

Like everything's about to go sideways again. Just like last year.

As I dressed, the scent of wet tile and mist-blunted light ambushed me, like a thief in the dark. For a moment, memory transported me back in time.

While still bent over my shoelaces, I returned to that night. I heard Temperance's voice in the echo of dripping water. My heart pounded like it'd burst my chest and the air in my lungs burned as though underwater. I froze like a rabbit in front of a speeding car, unable to move another inch. Thanks to all those sessions with Ms. Khan, I knew what to do.

Despite the chest pain, I tried measuring my breath. That proved impossible, so I focused on forcing my fingertips to recognize the flat, rough weave of my shoelace. Something unrelated, native to the present, to ground me. In the end, none of that saved me.

Coach Pickman did.

She squatted in front of the bench I sat on and peered up at me.

Speaking softly wasn't her way, but she lowered her typical volume, offering familiar words of encouragement.

"Come on, Morgenstern. You've got this."

I nodded, senses finally returning fully to the present. My fingers fumbled, and I hadn't taken so long to tie my shoes since grade school. However, I managed. Afterward, I sat up. She got on the bench with me and sat for a spell.

"I don't know what got into me, Coach."

"This isn't a big day. It's colossal. The last test before you're done here, yeah, but you feel like the field's got some unexpected terrain. Pay attention to everything you see today, Morgenstern. Like you're playing Gallows Hill, and they finagled that crazy cloaking psychic onto the court."

"What do you mean?" I blinked. "Why?"

"People overlook me sometimes, so I hear things. Can't say much. Movers and shakers around here are, well, moving and shaking. Stay alert."

The bell rang.

"Better move along." She nodded at the clock above the doorway. "Don't want to be late."

"Thanks, Coach."

CHAPTER ELEVEN

After the final bell, both classes waited in turns outside the lab. My detour to the gym meant I arrived at the end of the line. Professor Hawkins stood at the door, letting the third-years in two at a time. He made pairs with each student from a different class.

"Don't blame Professor DeBeer or me for the order or the pairs." He held up a document on school letterhead. "Trustee designation." I saw Andre Gauthier's signature alone at the bottom.

You're nervous. And you don't want to wear those magical monstrosities.

I sighed along with the inside voice and put the ear cuffs on. There was no way around it, even with Leo Pierce off the Board of Trustees for now. Maybe future students wouldn't get stuck under such draconian measures. I'd met plenty of folks who figured they'd gotten theirs, so improving the world for the ones walking after them wasn't important.

I grinned, sure I wasn't one of them. If I'd learned anything at all over the last few years, it was that kindness matters. Everyone's fighting a secret battle, and nobody wins alone.

Hal was the first one out of the lab, with Lee exiting practically on his heels. As he passed me in the hall, Hal held his hand up and gave me a fist bump.

Our hands made contact for too brief a time for him to convey much, but hope, fear, and exhaustion flooded his mind in equal measure. I got the impression that he hurtled toward a yawning chasm, unable to stop before the edge. After that came a bizarre representation of the lab's wall, covered with carvings of Abe Fairbanks's face. Words scrawled across the whiteboard. *He's watching.*

He must have used space magic to get that information. No wonder he looked exhausted.

"Head to the library, gym, or Creatives," Professor Hawkins instructed. "Or the infirmary, as needed."

Hal and Lee headed down the hall, but I didn't see where they ultimately went.

Logan went in with Bailey Overton next. She must have studied because it was only five minutes before she headed to the library. Logan nodded at me and Grace, who pressed her lips into a thin line. I wondered why.

Faith and Eston went after that, and they took half the allotted time. Kitty and Dorian stepped through the door, but not before he glanced over his shoulder and gave the rest of us waiting two thumbs up.

Hailey went in with Dylan. It felt like an eternity, waiting outside with Grace. After thirty minutes, it was finally our turn.

"After you," I said.

Inside, the benches were arranged in two rows. Professor DeBeer started Grace up front on the left and me in the back on the right. We moved along at a similar pace, looking at pictures and replicas of a range of magical items, from ancient curiosities to mergers with modern technology.

I felt confident marking down most of the answers. The only blank I drew was over the replica amulet with a moon on one side and a wolf on the other. After picking it up and turning it over in my hands a few times, I got it. An alliance amulet used to forge pacts between werewolf packs and vampires.

Grace and I reached our last stations simultaneously, which meant she stopped where I'd started, and I ended where she'd begun. I wondered how she managed to navigate that entire ordeal so calmly once I saw the item on the bench.

An old brass lamp. Familiar, too.

I blinked, hoping my hands would stop shaking as I reached for it. Director-General Rockport had assigned me the ear cuffs, which dampened ranged mind magic but intensified it through touch. Miss Dunstable had given me exactly the information I needed so I wouldn't jot the answer down without checking. Plus, there was no way Hector Hawkins hadn't recognized his mother's lamp when he added it to the practical. Had they planned this all along? Or was this another replica, fashioned in a fit of nostalgia and wishful thinking?

The only way to find out was by touching it. I was afraid. Professor DeBeer had apologized for her bias against extramagi, but she was watching. I swallowed, unsure of what to do next.

Another student must have already touched it. Rubbed it, even and become its master. Hal had been in here first, but Gamila couldn't have shown herself. If she had, the headmaster would have postponed the exam, the room overrun by staff and faculty. He probably thought it wasn't the real thing.

Maybe she was canny enough to hold back. I couldn't resist hesitating. Too much was at stake.

On the other side of the room, Grace cleared her throat and raised her hand. Professor DeBeer turned her back to help. I knew it was a cue; the only chance I was likely to get. I took it.

The moment my fingers made contact, I felt the hum of consciousness encased by magic and metal. I tucked it under my arm, then jotted the answer "djinn lamp" in the space for station number one.

Grace leaned over her paper but tilted her head up a little, brow furrowing as she stared at my arm. Then, she jerked her chin at the door. She'd cloaked it, of course.

With the lamp still tucked under my arm, I set my answer sheet on the teacher's bench and strode out the door.

Professor Hawkins nodded as I walked by but said nothing. Nearly breathless, I kept my pace steady and pedestrian down the hall. Why hadn't I turned to see where Hal had gone?

I poked my head into the library first, then the gym, and finally Creatives. He wasn't among the students I saw in any of those places. I didn't see Faith, either. With one hand, I removed my ear cuffs, trying to home in on them. After a moment, I was aware of Grace, keeping pace a few yards behind me on the opposite side of the hall. For a moment, I thought I sensed someone else too.

As if an exam wasn't stressful enough, it had to go and transform into a heist.

Hal could have been in the café, the cafeteria, or even his room. I let my feet go where they would, trusting mind magic to lead them in the right direction. That turned out to be down the ramp to the infirmary.

The desk in the waiting room was unoccupied. Muffled voices, raised more than normal, called out at regular intervals from one of the treatment rooms. I broke into a run, bursting through the door. A moment later, I stopped.

Nurse Smith and Ian were working as hard as they could. Not to save Hal, who was where I expected him to be. Andre Gauthier lay on a wheeled stretcher. He wasn't responding, not to chest compressions or rescue breaths. Nurse Smith looked up when I walked in.

"Thank the gods, someone from a medical family." He jerked his chin at the phone on the wall. "Call rescue. Magifinil overdose, adult male, Hawthorn Academy."

Magifinil blocks mind magic. That's why any attempt to read him bounced off.

It all made sense now. Andre had found the lamp and swapped it for the replica in the exam. He knew about Noah's gloves and signed our practical schedule.

Maybe Abe Fairbanks would kill to get the lamp. Andre Gauthier was prepared to die making sure he didn't.

"Not on my watch."

I called 911 and repeated the information Nurse Smith had given so he could keep working.

"Ian, keep compressions while we wheel. I'll give them the other emergency outside. Once he's in transport, we come back for our next patient."

They ushered the stretcher out, the door swinging shut behind them.

I glanced over to see Hal hooked up to tubing, like any other infusion. But something was different this time.

He sat propped up on the bed, his face an almost claylike shade of ashy brown. His eyes were open but dull somehow, like scuffed marbles.

At first, I thought the worst. But he blinked. From the bedside, Faith looked at my hands, eyes rimmed with red.

"Fumbled the play, huh?"

"No, Faith." I walked right up beside her. "I didn't, thanks to Grace."

"I don't see it." Hal breathed. "Don't see much of anything now."

"Look again." I set the lamp in Hal's lap, breaking the veil of umbral magic Grace had cast over it.

He blinked once more, squinting like he couldn't see clearly. But Faith recognized it immediately. She took his hands and placed them on the lamp.

"I need time," he said. "We don't have it."

"Why not?"

"Grandpa's off-campus, visiting Bubbe," Faith answered. "Nurse Smith went to get the man in charge. My tyrant of a father."

"Well, he's not here yet. If he wants to come in, he'll have to get through me."

I strode toward the door. Hal spoke as I pulled it open.

"He's got help. And a shield. You'll need an army."

"Dunno what for, but we've got one." Grace stood outside, but her statement confused me because she seemed to be alone.

I filled her in as I stepped out and closed the door. Behind me, Faith locked it.

"Figured he'd pull shenanigans." Grace sighed. "Thanks for coming, folks."

Grace waved a hand, and her umbral magic faded, coloring me impressed. She'd cloaked all the third-years, probably fetched them from the rooms I checked as she followed me out of the academic wing. Everyone but Dylan and Logan had their familiars with them. Arick, Lena, and Xan were there, too.

"You're skipping class?" I blinked.

Lena nodded.

"Worth it." Arick grinned.

"What can they do, hold me back another year?" Xan snorted.

"We can do far worse than that, my dear boy."

Lavinia Onassis stood at the bottom of the ramp to the infirmary. Her basilisk hissed as venom dripped from her fangs. The smile on the woman's face was pure poison.

"I've got her." I cracked my knuckles. "Burning off poison's a piece of cake."

"No." Lena pointed. "Get him."

"None of you stand a chance." He chuckled, low and intense. It'd been him then, on the cruise. "I'll block everything you throw at us until you surrender or die. Either way, I'm getting that lamp. Don't expect any help, either."

Mr. Fairbanks stepped out of the shadows. The first thing he did was set up a barrier behind us. I recognized it because I made one like it the night of the masquerade ball to hide Dorian and Xan from Lavinia. Mrs. Pierce leaned on one of his arms. On the other, he held the shield Hal had mentioned.

It wasn't shaped like any sort of conventional weapon, either. It was magical, a device that produced wards. I knew because he put an umbral one up right after the mind, so nobody would hear or see whatever they meant to do to us.

"You could be good little children and let us in." Mr. Fairbanks chuckled again. "We've already won."

"Huddle up, team."

Everyone did, not only my Bishop's Row folks.

"He's not bluffing," I said. "We need to get that device from him and have someone positioned to get around his home-grown mind barrier once the other wards go down."

"I'm not MVP for nothing," Dylan said. "I'll dodge my way past the baddies and get help."

"BS." Grace rolled her eyes. "It's me, and you know it. Umbral's the ticket out. I just need cover."

"Got that." Lee put his hand out. Lena, Xan, and Dylan stacked theirs up. I put mine on top and nodded.

"If you need a hand up, I'm here," Eston said.

"Air support," the twins said.

"Distraction detail." Kitty joined them in a three-way fist bump.

"I'm with them." Arick jerked a thumb at his squadmates. "How will Grace remember us once she's through?"

"Ear cuffs." Logan pointed at me. "They dampen mind energy. Put them on her."

We broke the huddle. I took them off and passed them to Grace. Mr. Fairbanks frowned as she put them on.

"Tiffany, keep them on their toes."

Mrs. Pierce waved a hand, looking like the magic she conjured took barely any effort. I knew from long experience that she was afflicted by resting boredom face. So maybe calling forth an ice storm out of thin air wasn't as easy as she made it look.

"Dracula's balls!" Dorian's look of horror confirmed my suspicions. "Dylan, a little help here."

They began banishing and good thing too. We might have all ended up sliding around on the tile defenseless if it iced over.

"Rush play, cover mid, go!" I called to my team.

Lena jumped out in front, hurling a poison orb at Tiffany Pierce. Lavinia raised a hand to banish it from across the room.

Xan tossed another orb right through Lavinia's line of sight and she ended up banishing that instead. Lena's orb continued on its path.

Tiffany waved her free hand and a wall of ice formed. Lena's orb bounced off. I sent a fireball streaking toward it. Abe knocked it aside with a mind blast. I had to banish it myself before it hit the nurse's desk and did more than smolder. The Overton's pigeons dove at his head but they turned aside at the last moment to avoid a poison orb from Lavinia. Julia took wing and banished it before it could land and do any more damage.

Somewhere in all that confusion, Grace must have cloaked herself. I couldn't see her or sense her presence, which meant the ear cuffs were doing their job. Despite all the banishing Dylan and Dorian did, some of Tiffany's storm hit the floor. My fireball had melted it, which meant Grace left visible footprints.

"Logan, Eston!" I pointed at the still smoldering desk, close enough to Grace's position to indicate without giving her away.

They doused it. Water flowed with enough depth and splashing to cover Grace's tracks. Eston's Labrador familiar cavorted in the puddles with Lune, further obfuscating Grace's path.

"Cut off the head," Abe said.

"Down!" Lee knocked me aside right before a purple-tinted icicle speared me in the chest. He winced in pain as it grazed his left arm. The wood orb he'd been conjuring fizzled out like Arick's on the boat. He tried conjuring again but couldn't because Lavinia was still standing. Lune dashed to his side and helped Scratch defend him from stray orbs and icicles.

"Ladies!" Logan called out. "Thread the needle. Go!"

Kitty held her hands up, fire blazing around them. The twins stood on either side, conjuring air that fed the flames. Her sphinx twined his tail around her ankle, and the fire blasted between Tiffany and Lavinia, a move I instantly felt slice through their dual conjuring. Our opponents immediately began rebuilding their link again, but it'd take time.

I had to get to Abe. If I didn't do it now, his allies would wear us out while he erected wards behind him with the shield. Grace must have been at the exit by then, or close enough that she'd arrive once I made my play.

This wasn't Bishop's Row. We had no protective ballistae, ankyr, or cestus. Coach Pickman's whistle wouldn't blow for time out. Scores were counted by incapacitation, and Lee had been lucky.

"Cover barrage!"

Xan, Lena, and Hailey conjured orbs and hurled them at Abe. He ducked them effortlessly of course. That was fine by me. I needed a distraction while moving safely between the ice and poison magi defending him. Abe wasn't in any danger at all. I knew exactly how much of an advantage mind magic gave. Lavinia didn't. Or maybe Xan's defiance was finally too much for her.

She snarled, conjuring and throwing faster than even Lee on his best day. Lena's size gave her a small target advantage plus the ability to hide behind the desk's wreckage. Hailey stopped conjuring orbs and channeled a whirlwind around herself to deflect the poison.

I pressed my advantage and took two steps toward Mr. Fairbanks, a tightly concentrated fire orb in one of my hands. He glanced at Tiffany.

She threw ice, but I melted it. She threw another, and the ice storm lost steam. She shook her head at Abe and continued with her storm-bringing. Lavinia hadn't paused her barrage, her son the focus of all her attacks now.

Xan faced them all head-on. When he had no orb to block with, he swatted her attacks back at her with empty hands. She didn't seem to run out of steam. Poison magi were immune to their toxin, but even a parent's was different enough to be dangerous.

"Stop this, Mom." If he'd been fatally dosed, Xan gave no outward indication. Still, I heard fear singing all around him. "Before someone gets hurt."

"You'll hurt before I'm through," she shrilled. "Pharmaka, don't hold back!"

Lavinia's familiar slithered and became a purple blur on the floor. Kitty saw and aimed a jet of flame, but too late. Arick tried lifting a floorboard in her way, but the basilisk scaled it like lightning. She struck at Xan's leg quicker than I thought possible.

Asceco was faster. The smaller green basilisk struck back. Fangs slashed and clashed, venom flying every which way.

"Move it, Morgenstern!" Xan called.

I moved forward again, wondering whether Mr. Fairbanks would put up a shield at the last minute. He only stood there, an unfathomably mild grin on his face.

"Move!" Dorian called while flinging ice.

It knocked Pharmaka aside as she was about to strike.

No matter what Lavinia threw at him, she couldn't bring Xan down. I'd lost count long ago of the orbs he'd deflected unarmed. Maybe he had an antidote or learned a way to transform her toxin into his. However he managed, his victory seemed assured although he hadn't delivered anything but defensive blows.

Xan made no mistakes. Not even morally in the heat of emotionally charged combat.

His familiar took a wrong turn.

"It's okay." Lavinia gave her son a gentle smile. "I'll buy you a new one."

She destroyed Xan with a single hollow stomp as her heel crushed Asceco's head. He dropped to his knees on the sleety floor, head bowed and sobbing.

Everything stopped, at least on the student side of the battle. Most of us had seen Leo give Doris to the kraken, but he'd done the same with Brand and had the excuse of paying a life debt.

Asceco's murder was sickening.

"I'm tired of all this drama." Abe brandished the shielding device. I felt a ward go up that separated familiars from their magi. "If any break through, I kill them. Unless you're ready to surrender."

"Never!" Dorian stood holding an ice orb, Julia above him, channeling poison into it. "Take that, sadistic bitch!" He launched it at Lavinia. It hit her squarely in the face and knocked her to the floor with a wet smack.

"I warned you." Abe sighed. "You should know better, Mr. Spanos."

He didn't use magic to attack. Instead, a tiny throwing dagger whipped through the air and hit the strix in the middle of her chest. Blood dripped, pattering on the floor.

I expected Julia to drop out of the air dead like Mercy. That didn't happen. She was a tougher older bird and had never forgotten her first magus's example. Julia refused to fall without a fight.

None of us humans had seen Tiffany Pierce's familiar, but I'd sensed some creature helping her create that storm. Julia knew more than I did. It was an ice dragonet with scales the hue of a polar bear's fur, hidden under her voluminous bleached blonde hair.

The dying strix controlled her descent and scratched the dragonet on the way down. It *cheeped* unhappily. The storm didn't disappear, but it abated somewhat, and Tiffany had to use more of her power to maintain it. Dylan kept banishing, countering the ice storm on his own.

Dorian scooped Julia up, then rushed to Xan's side where they sat huddled together. Lee joined them. Kitty, Eston, Arick, and the twins defended them from Lavinia's renewed attacks with a series of fire orbs, whirlwinds, and sheets of water.

"Now, Miss Morgenstern." Abe narrowed his eyes. "Let's finish this."

I strode forward this time, unhindered. Mr. Fairbanks, despite his apparent confidence, looked tired of all of this. Maybe using the shield device had sapped his energy. Perhaps Hal wished right now. Maybe luck was on my side this time.

It wasn't.

Abe's familiar flew at my face and clung to my forehead. I had no time to dodge the scarab's attack. I'd encountered it before and nearly lost myself in the process. I was only slightly less prepared that time.

I swatted at it with two conjures, solar on one side and fire on the other. I dazzled my own eyes and singed my eyebrows. Those attacks stopped short, blocked by wards.

I tried mind, but the insect only siphoned that. I couldn't remove it mundanely. Giving the scarab more points of contact with my skin would only let it into my mind faster.

A gentle breeze blew by my right cheek and brought with it a hint of sandalwood and the memory of a pair of deep brown limpid eyes. Hal had eyes like that.

He's gone.

"No." I knew that inside voice wasn't mine this time.

Yes. That must be why you thought of him just now.

I refused to believe it. When I left the room, Hal already had the lamp. Minutes had passed. There was no way he hadn't used it. Take that and choke on it, dissociation voice.

"Shields win." Abe let out that chuckle again. "I captured the queen. Check."

Behind me, my friends gasped, growled, and cried out in defiance. However, none of them besides Logan had any idea what was in store if I couldn't resist Abe and his scarab a second time.

Whatever gambit Hal had going with the lamp and his wishes, we needed it before I dissociated again and ended this battle in the most logical and definitive way possible.

Friends, foes. There's no difference. Burn them all.

That awful voice told me exactly what that was before beginning the work of separating my mind from my body. Of course, Abe would use his shield device to save his allies, their children, and whichever of my friends he thought he could break. The rest would all be victims, and me a scapegoat like every other extramagus bogeyman.

CHAPTER TWELVE

Face Your Death
Hal

I'd spent the last three years trying not to waste time but running out of it anyway. I should have known that if anyone could buy me more, it'd be Aliyah Morgenstern. I refused to squander her kindness.

I was out of more than time now. My energy was almost gone.

Rubbing the lamp felt downright Herculean. Seconds stretched out as it glowed and spewed smoke, then revealed my grandmother who I'd only ever seen in pictures—old ones.

"Hi, Nana Mila."

"Queen's Grace, Harold!" Her eyes reddened. "In my worst nightmares, I never imagined you in this state."

At first, this confused me. I remembered in time how shocking it must have seemed, seeing someone my age at death's door.

"I'd like my wishes now if you don't mind skipping formalities." I tried to grin. The look on Faith's face told me I'd managed a grimace. "I know the rules."

"Wish on, child."

"I wish for an audience with the Sidhe Queen."

"Done."

Faith blew me a kiss. The wooden walls and tiled floor of the infirmary melted like wax under a lit wick on fast-forward. I found myself in a long hallway paved in glittering dun stone. At the end stood a set of double doors, tall and gilt.

"Come along."

Grandma Mila took my hand and a step forward. Inwardly, I balked because my brain told me there was no way I'd make it even halfway to the doors.

My body had other ideas.

I strode forward, pacing right along with her. I hadn't had a day this good since I helped Aliyah shop for Logan's birthday. It made sense. I was in the Under, where I could breathe in the magic my body needed. So we made it to the door in a few moments, where my grandmother spoke to one of the guards.

"Announce us, please."

The guard hefted her staff and used it to hammer the door three times. It opened, and she turned her back on us to step through before speaking in a booming voice.

"Duchess Gamila Haddad-Hawkins, lamp-bound, accompanied by her grandson Harold Hawkins, lamp-holder and magus of space."

"Enter and state your business," a voice replied.

The guard stepped aside to reveal a room built of the same glittering stone but ornately carved. A long red carpet ran between a row of columns, which led to a dais. Atop it sat a throne flanked by knights in alabaster armor, one with a red helmet and the other blue.

The Queen herself had amber-hued hair that hung in thick waves over her shoulders almost to her waist. A crown graced her head, golden and studded with diamond, topaz, and garnet. Her robes were long, sheer fabric with a coppery metallic sheen overlaying deep sunset orange.

We paced forward until we stepped between two columns, adorned with sconces lit by solar magic. Nana Mila bowed, holding my hand tightly so I had to follow suit. I would have anyway, but she barely knew me. For all she knew I might have had horrid manners.

That made me more determined to let her know who I was because I still wasn't sure whether my plan would work. I kept my head bowed as I made my address.

"Your Majesty, thank you for allowing me the gift of your valuable time. I seek your permission before making my second and third wishes." I dared a glance up.

"Permission?" The Queen tilted her head. "Interesting. Why?"

"It requires your intervention, Majesty. Becoming a djinn."

"To what purpose? Power? Glory? Of all the people in Faerie, djinn have the least potential for these. Theirs is a life of service and sacrifice."

"I'm dying, Majesty, of a magical malady. My illness is writ in the very fiber of my being, and I already know wishes can't erase it. But my lineage is indelible too. It's the only way to save my life."

"Technically, you are correct. However, granting your request will not cure you in the mundane realm. You'll still suffer many of its hardships, although not fatally."

"I understand, Your Majesty." I nodded. "I can live with that."

"If I say yes, what will you do?"

"Pledge fealty to Your Majesty, and take my grandmother's place in her lamp after my third wish, so it continues in your service."

"That third wish, what will it be?"

"Justice. Too many I love suffer without it."

"*My* permission is yours. But know this, young magus. Bestowing a new mantle is a tandem effort between myself and His Majesty, and more from Duchess Gamila. If consent is important to you, his is as significant as mine."

I stood at the brink of despair. Somewhere in the fog of magic deprivation, I'd miscalculated.

My friends back in the mundane world were either already engaged in combat with senior magi or about to be. They needed one of my wishes to survive as surely as I did. I'd come to terms with death before holding the lamp was certain, but only as long as they continued.

Now, caught between saving my expiring life and all of theirs, the choice was clear.

"I will face my fate and do without to save my wife, my father, and my friends. Nana, I w—"

"His Majesty, King of Wood and Wild, Master of the Hunt, Husband and Peer to the Sun Court's Glory."

"Enter, Baelgreth." The Queen rose.

The air to my left stirred like an autumn breath, the one that takes the last leaf off the oldest oak in the forest at the fall of the year.

I studied the figure standing beside the queen. They were of a height, but night and day in most other respects. He wore a long black cloak with tattered edges over forest green traveling clothes. While the Queen went unarmed, he was girt with dagger and rapier.

"My love." He took her hands and kissed each of them in turn. "Forgive my hasty entrance. I couldn't ignore these strands of fate." He tilted his head at me.

"As I suspected. I agree. The fiber of his being also calls to me."

"Empathy. Forgiveness." The King grinned.

"Honor. Above all, bravery." The Queen nodded. "Perhaps this...collaboration...is practice for something else."

"Shall we, then?" He raised an eyebrow.

"We consent, young magus. Only one more thing needs doing to complete this magic."

"Go on, Harold. Make your wish."

"I wish to be a djinn, like my grandmother before me."

Nana Mila glowed. It seemed to come from within, as though every cell in her body became luminescent. Myriad colors, a shrouded rainbow, flowed out of her and toward the Monarchs on the dais. They each held out a hand, collecting the light between them. As it gathered, they each added to it, the King's contribution in swirls of green, blue, and purple and the Queen's red, orange, and yellow.

It reminded me of Bishop's Row, what I imagined would happen if everyone combined their orbs. Except the energy between them grew impossibly large, which transcended its appearance. Visually, it fit in their hands, but I sensed that its borders exceeded the walls of the throne room.

The Queen smiled down at me. Then, with the King, she aimed that massive orb at me. It didn't fly so much as roll forward.

All my hair stood on end, even the stubble on my head, which I'd shaved in November because I thought it'd be easier to manage. It hadn't grown back. A breath later, I felt it lifting and itching as it returned.

My feet left the stone-covered carpet as light, magic, and heat encased me. I remembered a lab experiment, one of Filberto Luciano's more daring ones done with a crucible. Maybe I understood it better now, from an unexpected perspective. I hung suspended in one, both my state and composition changing irrevocably.

I opened my mouth, unsure why until light and sound poured from it. I'd always been tone-deaf, but for the only time in my life, I sang perfectly. It made sense. I was in the middle of a miracle, after all.

"You deserve one, after making so many."

The Queen's voice didn't startle me. Her words did. Until scenes from my life paraded through my consciousness.

Grandpa Hiram on house arrest, eyes lighting up when I visited.

Dad in the headmaster's office, doubting his new job until I said I believed in him.

Showing Lee around Salem the day he arrived on campus.

Faith in the cafeteria, taking my hand for the first time.

Keeping Aliyah's secret.

Grace agreeing to beat me at Scrabble during that rocky first-year winter break.

Inventing devices with Logan.

Riding the train to Boston after Dylan's breakup, just to get him out of town.

Sitting with Darren after his familiar was poisoned.

Walking a nervous Eston to cheer squad tryouts.

Meeting Dorian in the bathroom to practice his stand-up routine.

Decorating the classroom door for Professor Luciano.

Proofreading Kitty's numerous college entrance essays.

Practicing with the Overtons in a mirror so we'd stop calling Xan by his old name.

Forgiving my mother when she promised to do better.

"And now, we empower you to make one more." My song, the memories, and the magic ended on the Queen's last word.

My feet came to rest on the floor. My Hawthorn Academy infirmary slippers were gone, replaced by my favorite brown loafers. I blinked, realizing that somehow the convalescent clothing I'd been stuck wearing over the last few months was replaced by the khakis, chambray button-down, bow-tie, and blazer I favored. Plus, they were comfortable again.

"Your Majesty." I took a knee, without any worry about whether I'd be able to stand later. "I pledge myself to your service, in fealty, and dedicate my service to my wife, Faith Fairbanks-Hawkins."

"Then you will remain in the Under, Harold Hawkins, doing the work of my Court as squire to Sir Frederick. Your wife will have leave to visit once your duties are established. Your term endures for one year and one day, with one exception—the moment it takes to retrieve the lamp currently occupied by your grandmother. You will transport it here immediately after," the Queen said. "You may rise and make your final wish."

"Nana, I want justice. For my family, friends, and those who would do them harm."

"As you wish."

The Queen snapped her fingers, and a portal opened. Through it, I saw the infirmary waiting room, much of it in ruins, the battle still raging. My grandmother held her hands out, brow furrowed and beaded with effort. Justice seemed to be a taller order than I'd expected.

When she lowered her hands, I felt myself move involuntarily through space, drawn into the portal, past the magi locked in combat, over Aliyah and Mr. Fairbanks as he uttered the word check.

I wanted to stop and help but couldn't. The lamp pulled me inexorably on through the door.

On the edge of the bed I'd almost died in, Faith's eyes widened. I saw myself reflected in them, not as I'd appeared in the Under, but as a plume of golden smoke flowing toward the lamp cradled in her arms. I took form.

"It worked." Faith held the lamp out to me. "Or it will once you take her place. I love you."

I leaned forward, bending to kiss her.

"I love you too. Go out now and help Aliyah. She's in serious trouble. See you soon."

The moment I touched the polished brass, I vanished with it and Nin, back to the Under.

CHAPTER THIRTEEN

Aliyah

"Checkmate, Dad." Faith stood in the doorway alone, hands empty. "Get your hooks off my friend."

"You're one of us, Faith. A Fairbanks. You can't erase that."

"That's Hawkins now. I'm erasing your victory, not myself."

I felt the hum of emotion from her, how it focused on her father with laser precision. Faith hadn't been present to fight her sister last year, but she was here now and done tolerating what her family did in the shadows.

"Sic him, Seth."

I never suspected Seth was the most loyal out of all our familiars, but his devotion in those moments was legendary. I knew he smelled the throwing knives up Abe's sleeve. I sensed his fear. He followed Faith's order immediately anyway, and that little dog saved my soul.

Sha are the size of chihuahuas, but they pounce like panthers. Wards might have protected the scarab from my magic, but they did nothing against the frenzy of its natural predator. Especially one bonded to a magus as righteously angry as Faith at that moment.

Seth held the scarab in his teeth without biting down. I felt indignation and fear coming off the insect and joy from Seth. This was what he was made for. He ran under a chair on the other side of the room, separating the critter from its magus. And from me.

That waking limb feeling came over me for the second time. I cried again, but I didn't let it stop me from reaching for the shield device still in Abe's hand. I winced and looked down to find my wrist impaled with one of his blades.

"Don't bring a fist to a knife fight."

Behind him, Grace made a zipping motion over her lips. She touched the device, and it vanished a second before she did.

"Don't stab fire magi." I winced, tears still streaming from my eyes as I conjured flames to stop the bleeding. "What did you say? We've already won. Be good parents and let us through?"

"The next one goes in your throat." He snorted.

"I'm an extramagus. You think I can't stop you?" I glanced at his seemingly empty hand and hoped the pain hid my bluff. "By the way, your shield's gone."

He looked for it and blinked, then opened his hand like most people who don't believe in anything they can't see.

The device wasn't missing, of course, only cloaked. It clattered to the floor and cut off the wards for real this time. He bent to retrieve it, but a wooden panel appeared out of nowhere and knocked it across the room.

"What happened here?" A pajama-clad Noah blinked blearily at the door of his borrowed apartment, surveying the damage. "Hurricane Hawthorn?"

Justice prevailed after that.

Grace's voice echoed back through the hall followed by answering footsteps a moment later. She led a crowd through, mostly faculty but also Nurse Smith, walking with Detective Ambersmith. I learned later he called her because the wards made him think Hal and Faith were missing.

Abraham Fairbanks tried covering for himself with his magic. But the Magifinil overdose was already logged, along with a journal on

Andre's person that detailed everything he'd observed as a trustee this year.

Plus, he'd forgotten who his allies were.

Xan's mother hit him with the same nullifying toxin she'd used on the dagger and Lee. She did it the moment she saw a Salem PD uniform. Because of her betrayal, he couldn't keep himself out of the police reports.

We all made statements that day, detailing crimes like assault, threats, and killing familiars. Lavinia Onassis made the confession that ended up putting him away for crimes against extrahumanity, Geneva Convention-level stuff. Two of his planned wishes involved genocide. She gave them all the details in exchange for extradition of her case to Greece where she had the protection of her title, of course.

Tiffany Pierce didn't bother lying either. Since she hadn't technically done anything illegal and denounced the familiars' killing, she was off the hook with the police. The school stripped her of her title and alumni status, then banned her from campus for life.

Leo remained at the Danvers Sanitarium in their aggression wing. Crow joined him soon after. Mavis told me he would have been in High Extrahuman Security since he already had a record. Her mom was all set to let him rot because he'd squealed on Lavinia about the knife. Paolo Micello intervened and pulled some strings to get him a chance at rehabilitation instead.

We heard about most of this during the last week on campus, but were largely uninvolved because Ember's clutch hatched the morning after the battle. I was in the infirmary having my dressings changed when it happened.

A cacophony of peeping, cheeping, cooing, and blooing sounded in the hall and grew closer by the second. It woke Xan and Dorian, who'd slept there overnight. Logan burst through the door, followed by Dylan with Gale crooning on his shoulder.

"You're never going to belie—" Dylan got interrupted by what looked like a cloud of scaly wings and tails.

They streamed into the room in a flock, wheeling overhead as they separated. Ember dived first, puffing her skinny chest out proudly. Logan laughed.

"She says, 'I'm so awesome, I made all of these.'" He blinked as something crashed into his head. "Ow."

A little teal dragonet clung to his hair. It craned its neck over Logan's forehead and peered into his face upside-down.

"Cheep?"

"Buddy? That was a big bump. Are you okay?" Logan held his forearm out in front of him at chest level, horizontally.

"Cheep!" The dragonet glided down and hopped from one foot to the other on his new perch. "Cheep cheep!"

"Right, I get it. Buddy's your name, and you're hungry."

Nurse Smith taped the bandage over my wound. "I'll get them some snacks. No fish heads allowed in here, though."

"Um, guys?" Xan sat with his hands over his head, which a green dragonet dived at repeatedly. "What do I do?"

"Let her land." I grinned. "She likes you."

He lowered his arms, and the green dragonet went right for his head, clinging in his unkempt curls and cooing contentedly.

"Uh, I guess she's Percy." Xan looked over at Dorian, who'd pulled the covers over his head.

"Not again," he sobbed. We all huddled around his bed.

"Hey." Xan rubbed his back through the sheet. "What do you need?"

"I don't even know anymore." He sniffled. "Space, I think."

"Okay." Xan nodded. "You heard the man."

We moved to the waiting room, where Nurse Smith left a tray of fish pellets on a table. The dragonets ate while we sat and watched them. Ember flapped and hissed at any who got too greedy. She wanted to make sure her children got enough. Gale strutted around the tray without eating, admiring his offspring. A pair of yellow dragonets split their pellets and shared with each other. I guessed that they were solar. A sleek gray one examined each morsel before eating it. I also saw a blue one, a different shade than Gale and with aquatic looking fins. Buddy kept trying to pass pellets to a little white dragonet, but he *cheeped* and turned his back. He hadn't had a single bite.

"No more pining." Dorian stepped out of the doorway and took a pellet from Buddy. The white dragonet accepted it from him. "I get it. You need me." He cradled him in his arms and fed him another pellet. "His name's Rime. And yeah, he's ice."

In the office, I almost called Bubbe to examine Ember's new family. Although the hospital had discharged her, she needed three weeks at Oaken Acres Rehab. Dad came to look them over. He was the Morgenstern at the extraveterinary practice now. Bubbe already said she'd retire, unsure she'd be able to handle struggling creatures with her weakened right hand.

I brought the unbonded hatchlings to visit anyway, after getting permission from the staff. Petra was visiting with Andre in the lobby at the time, so they came with me. The blue water dragonet flew backward in front of Petra, cheeping.

"Hello there, little one." She smiled. "No, I haven't had a companion in years. Yes, I'd love to." The dragonet landed on her shoulder. "Her name's Marina, by the way."

Bubbe was in her room when we got there. She bonded with one of the yellow ones right away, and it flew to and fro, fetching little items for her. His name was Sonny.

"Don't look now, Aliyah." She glanced over my head. "I think you've got a new friend."

She was right. The other half of that pair told me her name was Dawn. Bubbe said that sometimes extramagi ended up with two familiars. That explained what happened to Dylan later.

"This one won't leave me alone." He sighed over the gray dragonet sleeping on his shoulders. "Isn't one enough? Gale keeps me on my toes."

"Gust is mild, though," Logan said. "Maybe she'll be a good influence on him."

The entire third year class went to the science fair for Hal's entry. His Neshmet chair won first place, and MIT was fine with him taking a gap year. Faith carried the blue ribbon and the news to him on her first visit to the Under.

He'd always need the chair in the mundane world, and his magic would wear down without regular visits to the Under, but as a djinn he had numerous reasons to visit. He could live a full life, although Faith insisted there was no way she was giving birth to thirteen kids.

We worried about how he'd graduate. Hal's agreement with the Queen meant he couldn't leave the Under. Instead of the lobby, Gamila suggested we hold the ceremony in the auditorium. Everybody thought it was a way to accommodate Noah since the room was sunproof. On the day, while the rest of us lined up in caps and gowns, ready to walk between the seats and across the stage, a portal opened beside the podium. Apparently, there was a thin spot in the barrier between worlds up there. Hal smiled down at us from the other side.

Hiram handed his diploma through. The sound of our applause must have carried because I saw the tears on his face as he waved before the portal closed. The rest of the ceremony proceeded in alphabetical order, beginning with Kitty Byers and ending with Lee Young.

The diploma felt oddly light in my hand, as though the education it represented wasn't such a big thing. Maybe that was right. The books, labs, and exams were only a small fraction of my lessons at Hawthorn Academy.

Walking off stage, literally and figuratively between all the friends who'd been with me on this journey through school felt like a fitting end to this story of mine.

The thing about knowledge is this. It's a lot like love, which exists all around us in infinite forms. Learning is endless, as long as you're brave enough to seek it out and let it in.

The End

Read on for an epilogue.

EPILOGUE

Dear Noah,

How's everything going across the pond? As I write this, you only left a month ago, but it feels like a year and a day. So much has happened.

I went to a Piercing Whispers show. Cadence is rocking on vocals, no offense. Can you believe Arick commuted from Norway all summer to gig with them? Carick is still a thing, and it gives them some nice energy on stage. They picked up one of Azrael's cousins as their new guitarist, Winnifred. She's pretty good.

Hawthorn held a big alumnus meeting. Hiram stepped down as headmaster, so Hector's doing the job for real now. Plus, they selected three new trustees. Hiram himself, of course. Old Grandpa Ambersmith. And wait for it...

Bubbe! She's sick of retirement already, so it's good for her. She's excited because they already voted in some changes. Students have to be magi but can attend if they're also changelings, vampires, or somehow get a magic shifter item. That's happening way more often now for some reason. All the vampires they let go last year got offers to come back. Zeke asked me to thank you for fixing that desk lamp in his apartment. The solar energy was on the fritz for decades.

Logan's mom said she wanted nothing to do with the Menagerie anymore so she sold it and moved to Hawaii. Petra flew us all out with a lawyer and got Logan and Elanor their fair share of the proceeds. Petra ended up with a share too. Dad made sure the more docile critters were adopted, but there were a whole bunch that were too big or traumatized to find homes. Petra and Logan used their shares to buy a farm in Methuen and moved them there. Dad's got visiting privileges. We'll have to go up there next time you're in town. It's beautiful.

Grace is engaged. She asked Azrael, and they're getting married next year. State Of Grace has taken off too, gone international already. You probably already knew that. I helped her pack up a suit for shipping. The label had your address in Oxford. Most of her sales outside the US are from the UK.

Dorian's coming to PPC with the rest of us. He said it was his last choice, but he looked way too happy when he got his acceptance letter. He's majoring in Extrahuman Law if you can believe that. I met his parents again on a campus tour. They're almost as funny as he is, and great people too. Xan was with them. Reminds me of how our folks were with Logan. So it turns out we're not the only magi with decent parents.

I decided on Alternative Therapies for my major, like Faith. We're already planning our schedules so we can be lab partners. Doctor Klein's an adjunct so we'll be taking her classes next year for sure. Logan's in Extraveterinary. He got all twelve of his textbooks last week and read them already. Brianna's in Social Work. Bar's in Law and Contracts. Lee's undecided but leaning toward Ecology. Izzy's in Psychic Professional Studies. Kitty and Eston ended up in Germany at Black Forest University for Magipsychic Chemistry.

The Overtons took a gap year to travel internationally, and their first stop is a visit to the Black Forest for Oktoberfest. You'll probably see them around eventually, too. They're making a travel blog for magi based on major events. College-level Bishop's Row championship games are near the top of their list. I expect you and Dylan to make it that far, so don't slack at practice. I hope he's been showing you a good time. If not, tell him to call me, and I'll badger him until he does.

In your last message, you asked if I'd heard from Hal. That's a delicate subject, and it comes with a small request. The Queen's had him on some type of scouting mission with a knight you might remember from a few years back. Fred Redford. They're looking for an item, something extremely important to the King. Faith says he can't tell anyone more than that. Even with his space affinity and all the dowsing, he's not making any progress.

So, he's asked all of us to keep an eye out, wherever we are. He says the graduation ceremony's giving us a connection for a while, even through the barrier between worlds. So, he'll be able to pinpoint it if we've seen the item. Whatever it is. Unfortunately, he's under a ban and can't say what.

Logan's got some ideas. Since it's for the King and an artifact, he deduced that it must have big Unseelie energy. He guesses the Queen might already have the Seelie equivalent. Also, either the item is dangerous, or dangerous folk want it. Her Majesty wouldn't send a seasoned redcap knight along when his squire could have done all the work on his own unless she thought Hal needed muscle.

I guess it's never a bad idea to go through life with our eyes wide open anyway.

All my love,
Aliyah

Free bird? Don't make me laugh.

I'm Mavis Merlini and I want out. Of my shady family, this rowdy school, maybe even the world.

My brother got kicked out of Gallows Hill School for inciting mermaid violence. I'm determined to cut out all distractions and be the first of my six siblings to actually graduate. Which means living on campus and ignoring my extroverted roommate.

All my plans are doomed to failure when a goth lion shifter in a trench coat drops his feather. Of course I pick it up. It's shiny and I'm a raven shifter. I swear I meant to give it back. But now it's magically bonded to me and I can't. Now I've got obligations to a Faerie Monarch on top of everything else. And if I shirk them, I'll spend a hundred years in his dungeon.

Can I soar through this double life, or will I end up failing to launch?

Grab your copy today!

AUTHOR'S NOTES

Hello, Dear Reader.

I'm writing this with that tight sensation around my eyes. The one that always comes with leaky eyes. I'll be okay, this happens every time I write The End on a series. Still, saying goodbye to a main character is never easy.

Authors put characters through unforgiving paces, plotting obstacles at their feet every time we sit down at our keyboards. For the past eleven months, I've wondered whether some cosmic author out in the ether sits at their desk wincing at what they've typed. The way things have gone, I imagine his name is Chuck Shurley. If you're also a *Supernatural* fan, you might agree.

Aliyah's 2020 wasn't the same as ours, but it was the roughest ride I've sent her on so far. Some of her friends still have things to do in future books. You'll see at least one in Gallows Hill, which is the next series in the Revealed World. But for now, Aliyah Morgenstern is contented, and off being her best self.

I wish the same for you.

With gratitude,

D.R. Perry

GLOSSARY

People

- **Changeling**- A mortal child of either one or two faerie parents. Most changelings choose a monarch sometime in their twenties, although some do it earlier than they have to.
- **Dampyr**- The mortal offspring of two vampires. They aren't as rare as many suspect, although because their blood is exceptionally sustaining to vampires, they keep their status secret. Dampyr sometimes have magic or psychic powers that work unreliably.
- **Faerie**- A term used to describe either a changeling who has tithed to a monarch and spent a year and a day in the Under or the pure creatures such as Gnomes and Pixies who were created by the king and queen.
- **Ghost**- A dead person with unfinished business becomes a ghost. If a mortal makes a contract before death, that gives them unfinished business and lets them linger. When ghosts finish their business, they move on, but no one knows where they go from here.
- **Magus**- A mortal who can use magic. Magic comes from

energy in the world. Most magi can only use one type of magic. However, a rare few can do more than one kind. Those are called extramagi.

- **Merfolk**- People who can live on land with legs or in the sea with fins and tails. They only emerged from the ocean after the Big Reveal and are still extremely rare outside of harbor towns.
- **Psychic**- A mortal with psychic power. Psychic ability comes from a person's own body and mind.
- **Vampire**- An unliving person who drinks blood to survive and enhance their abilities. Only regular mortals, psychics, and magi can get turned into vampires. Shifters, changelings, and faeries won't turn, and most of those won't survive an attempt.
- **Shifter**- A mortal who can take an animal's shape. Shifters have one form, with coloring similar to what they have while human. They usually have an enhanced sense while human-shaped, which goes along with their animal. For example, an owl shifter might have keen eyesight and a wolf shifter, a great sense of smell.

Shifter Varieties

- **Dragon**- The only shifters who can see both magic and psychic abilities, though only while shifted. The most powerful ones can partially shapeshift. Dragons are immortal and reproduce infrequently. There are so few of them since the Reveal that they've started taking other magical shifters as mates.
- **Kelpie**- A magical shifter who gets their abilities from an enchanted faerie pelt that bonds with their soul. The Kelpie pelts were created by the Goblin King, so they have Unseelie energy and restrictions. A Kelpie's animal form is a horse. Families pass the pelts down through generations,

and part of each ancestor lives on to help their descendants.
The ancestors can get distracting, however.

- **Selkie**- A magical shifter who gets their abilities from an
  enchanted faerie pelt that bonds with their soul. The Selkie
  pelts were created by the Sidhe queen, so they have Seelie
  energy and restrictions. A Selkie's animal form is a seal or
  sometimes a sea otter. They can use water magic as long as
  they wear the pelt. Families pass the pelts down through the
  generations, and part of each ancestor lives on to help their
  descendants. The ancestors can get distracting, however.
- **Tanuki**- A magical shifter with enhanced speed and the
  ability to see all types of magic while shifted. They are also
  the only creatures who can manipulate luck, causing it to
  turn from good to bad or the other way around. They stop
  aging if they own a charm infused with luck from humans.
  Very few of those charms exist, having been either used up
  during the Reveal or locked away.

Powers

- **Air magic**- The power to conjure, control, and banish wind
  or air.
- **Earth magic**- The power to conjure, control, and banish
  earth, sand, or rock.
- **Empathy**- A psychic power to sense and influence emotions
  in other people.
- **Fire magic**- The power to conjure, control, and banish flames.
- **Ice magic**- The power to conjure, control, and banish ice.
- **Lightning magic**- The power to conjure, control, and
  banish lightning.
- **Poison magic**- The power to conjure, control, and banish
  poison. Each magus has a slightly different type of toxin
  they produce. Some are even antidotes to others.
- **Precognitive**- A psychic power to foretell future events.

- **Spectral magic**- the power to conjure, control, and banish light.
- **Spectral Affinity**- A trait some spectral magi have that makes them charismatic and believable.
- **Summoner**- A psychic power that lets the user make contracts with pure faeries, letting the summoner call them in times of need. Each creature has an anchor, some item symbolizing the bond. Mastery of summoning takes decades of study, which is why the most powerful are either vampires or past middle age.
- **Seelie**- The Sidhe queen's court. The Seelie way is about following the letter of the law, even when it's hard or cruel. They have a hard time reconciling faerie rules with the new mortal laws since the Big Reveal.
- **Solar Magic**- The power to conjure, control, or banish sunlight. Some of the most powerful practitioners can find hidden objects or discover long-kept secrets.
- **Solar Affinity**- A trait some solar magi have that makes them beacons for coincidence.
- **Space magic**- The power to move the self or objects instantly across distances. Some can even move other people.
- **Space Affinity**- This space power comes with an ability to locate people or things important to the magus.
- **Telekinesis**- A psychic power that moves objects.
- **Telepathy**- A psychic power to read minds.
- **Tithe**- The process of pledging to either the queen or king, making a changeling choose to be either Seelie or Unseelie.
- **Umbral magic**- The power to conjure, control, and banish shadows and veil or camouflage objects or people.
- **Umbral Affinity**- A trait some umbral magi have that makes them difficult to remember without psychic ability, faerie magic, or a shifter pack bond.
- **Undeath magic**- The power to conjure, control, and banish unliving energy.

- **Unseelie**- The Goblin king's court. The Unseelies bend the rules and often navigate mortal society more easily than their Seelie counterparts.
- **Water magic**- The power to conjure, banish, and control water.
- **Wood magic**- The power to conjure, banish, and control wood. It takes extreme power to influencing a living plant.

Creatures

- **Basilisk**- A venomous serpent that also has poison magic.
- **Dragonet**- A tiny dragon-like creature, always associated with one or more element which powers their breath attacks later in life. They have scales but are warm-blooded like birds. Most don't get much bigger than a small cat.
- **Familiar**- A magical or mythical creature who makes a bond with a magus.
- **Gryphon**- A chimera which has the head of a bird and hindquarters of a predatory mammal. They come in several combinations of base species, and habitat influences their choice in magi to bond with.
- **Karkus**- A crab that can change its shape. They're said to be the offspring of the crab that pinched Hercules as he battled the Hydra.
- **Lightning Bird**- A familiar from South Africa with an affinity for lightning. Its beak can jump-start a car.
- **Mercat**- A shapeshifting feline with fur for land and scales in the water. They can live in lakes, rivers, or in the sea as well as on land. They must never completely dry out, or they will die.
- **Moon Hare**- A magical rabbit that gets power from its particular moon phase. They commonly bond with umbral magi.
- **Pharaoh's Rat**- These natural predators of dragon shifters are the size of ferrets and resemble a mongoose with more

fur. They have an affinity for space magic and can use it on occasion.

- **Pigeon**- Not as mundane as most think, some pigeons have an uncanny sense of direction due to their affinity for air magic.
- **Pricus**- An aquatic goat said to be descended from Capricorn. They can warp time even better than Gnomes.
- **Pure Faeries**- Creatures who spring to life from magical sources in the Under. They are genderless, and their type and ability depend on place of origin. They're associated with only one court, although they will work together to defeat a common enemy.
- **Sand Cat**- A feline that lives in the desert, able to go for weeks without water. Earth magic lets them do this.
- **Sha**- A magical desert dog from Egypt. Sha are the size of mundane toy breeds with short hair and small pointy ears. They could pass for mundane except for their blue tongues. They are attracted to anything undead.
- **Sphinx**- A magic cat with an affinity for fire. The reason they're hairless is that they're resistant to flames.
- **Strix**- A venomous owl with an affinity for poison. Female striges have rounded tufts on their heads, while males have pointed ones.
- **Sumxu**- A lop-eared cat found only in northern China. They are masters of camouflage and have an affinity for several kinds of magic.

Places

- **The Academy**—Something between a community college and a military academy for extrahumans, the Academy is geared toward helping extrahumans who don't play well with mortals get ready to join a blended society. It's got divisions for learners of all ages, though they are housed separately.

- **Cherry Blossom School**- A dojo geared toward teaching extrahumans self-restraint, meditation, and how to temper their enhanced physical abilities with more mundane skills. It's been around for close to a hundred years, run by the Ichiro family. Mundane classes used to be offered as a front but now are a separate division.
- **Ellicot City Magitechnic**- A prep school for magi and psychics specializing in magipsychic technology. It's located outside Baltimore.
- **Gallows Hill School**- Traditionally for shifters, this prep school in Salem recently opened its doors to changelings and other extrahumans not categorized as magi or psychics.
- **Hawthorn Academy**- A preparatory school for magi in Salem. Its campus is in the space between the mortal realm and the Under, giving it unrivaled privacy. They specialize in teaching familiar magic.
- **Providence Paranormal College**- A school founded just one year after Brown University and located right in its shadow. Providence Paranormal used to admit only magi and psychics, but it's been accepting all types of extrahumans ever since Henrietta Thurston became headmistress. There has been trouble since then for students and faculty, leading people to believe dissenters are sabotaging the school.
- **Trout Academy**- A prestigious preparatory school for changelings with magic, recently open to magi and magical shifters. Its campus is located in South County and has been operating in some form or another since Rhode Island Colony was founded.
- **The Under**- The faerie realm. It's been divided into two parts ever since the Sidhe Queen and the Goblin king split up thousands of years ago. Mortals don't age in the Under, but it's a dangerous place for them to be. Getting lost means never being seen again, and it's easy to get indebted to

something nasty while trying to get through or out of the Under.

- **Wolf Messing Prep**- An institute for psychics to learn to control their skills before heading to college.

Events

- **The Big Reveal**- The term used for the 1990s, when the world discovered magic was real and extrahumans existed. The decade was marked with fear as everyone adjusted to the changes. Since the 21st Century, law and technology work for both humans and extrahumans.
- **Boston Internment**- A reaction by Boston government officials to the disappearance and suspected trafficking in extrahumans, especially shifters. All registered extrahumans in Boston lived on barges for close to a month under guard by the Boston Police. The traffickers got their hands on some magical gadgets, rendering the protection useless. Few survived.

THANK YOU!

Thank you for reading! If you loved this book, please leave a review. You can find my other work by clicking the links below, going to **my website** or visiting my **Author Central page**.

Providence Paranormal College

Bearly Awake (Book 1)

Fangs for the Memories (Book 2)

Of Wolf and Peace (Book 3)

Dragon My Heart Around (Book 4)

Djinn and Bear It (Book 5)

Roundtable Redcap (Book 6)

Better Off Undead (Book 7)

Ghost of a Chance (Book 8)

Nine Lives (Book 9)

Fan or Fan Knot (Book 10)

Hawthorn Academy

Familiar Strangers (Book 1)

Acting in Kindness (Book 2)

Fire of Justice (Book 3)

Learning to Give (Book 4)

Light of Equality (Book 5)

Worthy Lives (Book 6)

Mind of Distinction (Book 7)

Speaking with Care (Book 8)

True Dedication (Book 9)

Gallows Hill Academy

Year One: Sorrow and Joy (Book one)

Year Two: Silver and Gold (Coming soon)

For other books by DR Perry please see her Amazon author page.

CONNECT WITH THE AUTHOR

Website: https://www.drperryauthor.com/

Join her newsletter!

Find more of D.R. Perry's books on Amazon.